# THE PAGAN BLESSING

## Phyllis Gebauer

THE VIKING PRESS · NEW YORK

First published in 1979 by The Viking Press
625 Madison Avenue, New York, N.Y. 10022

Published simultaneously in Canada by
Penguin Books Canada Limited

LIBRARY OF CONGRESS CATALOGING IN PUBLICATION DATA
Gebauer, Phyllis.
The pagan blessing.
I. Title.
PZ4.G2886PAG  [PS3557.E25]  813'.5'4  79–12880
ISBN 0–670–20972–4

Printed in the United States of America
Set in Linotron Garamond

# THE VIKING PRESS INC
### 625 MADISON AVENUE, NEW YORK, N. Y. 10022

## *Review Copy*

TITLE      **THE PAGAN BLESSING**

AUTHOR      Phyllis Gebauer

PRICE      $9.95, 244 pages

PUB. DATE      September 24, 1979

*Kindly send us two clippings or notification of broadcast of your review of this book.*

*For Fred*

# THE
# PAGAN
# BLESSING

# prologue

In the summer of 1276 a Spanish duke and his despondent young bride set off for the shrine of Saint James, seeking a cure for his lordship's humiliating affliction. Being well over seventy, Don Luis could accept his loss of memory, occasional stumbling, and incessant drooling, but this other . . . *por Dios,* that was something else again. Thus his pilgrimage to Santiago de Compostela and his entry one day into a sundappled oak grove.

At once, the old duke leaned from his litter.

"There," he quavered, pointing a bony finger at a huge tree in the center of the grove. "Quick! Set up my tent."

"But your grace, it's not yet noon," his squire protested.

"Time? Who cares about time? It's urges I'm concerned about. Urges!"

As the squire hurried off, Doña Anita, the duke's young bride, laid a trembling hand on her husband's forearm.

"Can it be true?" she whispered. "Does my lord finally feel an eventful stirring?"

The old man cackled obscenely. "Look around. Pagan ruins. This will be the place. I can feel it."

Doña Anita moved her hand elsewhere. "Oh, my lord," she breathed. "So can I."

The following morning a weak-kneed Don Luis flipped back his tent flap.

"*Vivan los célticos!*" he cried to his astonished retinue. "My pilgrimage is at an end. Never again will I depart from this oak grove."

And according to legend he never did, siring in the course of his stay eight husky sons and founding the village he called Amor Milagroso.

Unfortunately, soon after the duke was laid to rest, the citizens of Miraculous Love moved from the oak grove atop the hill down to a secluded cove on the shores of the Firth of Pontevedra. The way they explained it, the salt water offered them fish while the oak grove . . . well, what could they get up there but acorns and something in the air that made them feel good?

Thus no shrine was erected amid the oak trees, and for centuries no pilgrims, religious or otherwise, included the village on their itineraries. Then in the summer of 1975 an ex-fisherman named Benito Bazán found something in that grove that put Amor Milagroso in touch with its long-lost heritage. . . .

# PART I

# chapter 1

Head down, arm cradling his precious burden, Benito bounded down the hill, zigzagged through the vineyard, leaped a low stone wall, and angled across the cabbage patch. At last, arriving at the yard, he darted behind an apple tree and peered cautiously out from behind its trunk.

Good. The yard was deserted. Concepción hadn't gotten up early from her siesta to feed the chickens or slop the pigs. But she could be out at any second. He had to hurry. Hide what he'd found and be off about his chores.

Yet where to hide it? In the barn? The grain shed?

No. The box had to be out of sight, out of reach, dead and buried.

Of course. Bury it.

Sprinting to the barn, he grabbed a spade and ran back to the cabbage patch. Luck was with him. The pasture next to his was still deserted. Yet even if his neighbor Andrés Rabal should return, Benito's digging among the plants would seem perfectly natural. So the only problem was how to mark the spot so he could find it again.

He scanned the field. Every plant looked the same as the next. As did the rows. How to pick one and remember? He thought for a moment, then brightened. Of course. That was it. June twenty-first. The day his life changed for the better. With a triumphant smile he counted twenty-one rows from the barn, six cabbages from the edge of the field, strode forward, set down the box, and began to dig.

A pity he couldn't share his discovery with his wife. A pity she looked on things so differently. Yet wasn't that how Nature intended it? Except in bed, a man and a woman were supposed to go their separate ways. So it was only natural Concepción take care of the house, and he, the important things outside of it.

The hole deep enough for his purpose, Benito threw down his spade and wiped his brow with the sleeve of his shirt. He'd worked hard that afternoon; he'd have to be careful not to appear overly tired or Concepción would ask questions. If she did and he wavered, told her what he'd found, she'd insist he get rid of such heathen images right away. Perhaps surrender them to Father Juan. Even if she agreed that Benito had the right to sell them, she'd make sure the money would be used for better seeds, a new roof, winter clothing. She had right on her side, of course. There were so many things they needed. And a replacement for his shipwrecked fishing boat, the *A Mi Gusto*, wasn't one of them. . . .

Benito sighed, and squatting before the carved wooden box, raised the lid for a final look. There they were, nestled in what looked like decaying burlap: two golden statues that would more than pay for another fishing boat. On impulse, he lifted one of them out. Some fifteen centimeters high, it was the statue of a naked man standing with his head thrown back, his feet apart, his organ thrust skyward.

What a little braggart, Benito thought, then noticed that out in the sun the statue didn't seem to shine as much as it had back in the cave. *Maldita sea!* Was there a chance the gold wasn't real? A chance his treasure was worthless?

He rubbed a callused finger over the smooth metal. How cold it was and how strange to the touch. Like a throbbing fish, fresh from the sea. Yet the gold was different from that on the Jesús above the altar in the Amor Milagroso church. Maybe because this statue was very, very old. Yes, that was it. This statue was antique. Which meant it was even more valuable than he thought. One didn't see work like this anymore. Not even in the finest shops in Santiago de Compostela. Look at those little eyes, those ears, that grin. But then, what man wouldn't be grinning with equipment like that? Why, the little fellow's rod was almost as big as his forearm.

Benito chuckled and, still holding the man, reached for his golden companion. She, too, was smiling, but instead of standing up straight, she was bent over backward. He stroked her rounded breasts and arched belly, aware of a stirring inside his trousers. What a little tease, he thought, with her legs apart, a skirt that barely covered her . . . *Dios mío*, there was even a hole there. About the same size as . . . could it be if he put the two of them together, the man's—

"Benito, what on God's earth are you doing out here among the cabbages?"

Startled, he hunched forward. Tried to pull the figures apart.

Concepción moved around in front of him. "Benito, I asked you . . ." She paused, gaped at his fumbling hands. "*Mi madre,* what are you doing with yourself?"

"Hold your tongue, woman," he muttered, dropping the interlocked figures into the box and banging shut the lid. "Don't trouble yourself with things that don't concern you."

"It's not my concern when my husband crouches in a field like a lovesick cat?"

Benito's eyes moved from black shoes to black stockings. Then up a black skirt to a black blouse and, above that, a grim face framed by a black kerchief.

"See to the chickens, woman," he said. "While you were sleeping, that crippled fox came down again from the oak grove. If it hadn't been for me . . ."

He stopped, remembering the hoe he'd dropped at the entrance to the tunnel. Ay, *caray!* That could mean trouble. As soon as Concepción went away, he'd have to climb up that hill and get it. Because the cave wasn't only a place where there was hidden treasure. Judging from the cardboard boxes he'd seen stacked along the walls, El Chavo the smuggler was using it for a hideaway. . . .

"Yes?" Concepción prompted. "If it hadn't been for you?"

"The chickens, woman. See to the chickens."

"As soon as you tell me what you're doing."

"Nothing."

"Digging a hole is nothing? And what's that?" Pointing to the box.

"That, too, is nothing."

"Ay, Benito . . ."

He sighed. Got to his feet. "All right, then; it's a treasure."

"A treasure! What kind of treasure?"

"What does it matter what kind of treasure?" he cried, in the time-honored Galician way of answering a question by asking one. "The important thing is, it must be kept a secret."

"I see. This is something fit only for the eyes of your friends at the café." She sniffed. "Surely there couldn't be anything of value in a worm-eaten box like that."

"That's where you're wrong. Anyone experienced in the world would know a box like that could contain something truly magnificent. A holy relic, perhaps. Or jewels. Maybe even a pair of golden statues."

Concepción looked at him with interest. "And where did you find this thing?"

"What does it matter where I found it? You ask more questions than a *Guardia Civil*."

At that, man and woman faced one another in icy silence. Then the woman shrugged, turned on her heel, and started toward the house.

The man watched her go, knowing from the way she walked, the angle at which she held her head, that he'd hurt her.

He cleared his throat. Called her name.

She turned, stood waiting, eyes on her shoe tips.

He hesitated. Was she standing so humbly on purpose? Damn these women. A man could never tell.

He sighed, wondering what his friends at the café would do in such a situation. Surely he wasn't the only man in Amor Milagroso who continually yielded to his wife. But then, not many wives were like Concepción, who felt she had to be a partner in everything. Except in bed, of course, where she lay passive and unprotesting as any decent woman should.

"Were you going to say something?" she asked.

"I was going to tell you about the box. I found it up in the oak grove. There's a cave . . . you wouldn't have believed it."

He told her how he'd been hoeing the cabbages, caught sight of the crippled fox, chased him up the hill. Only to see him plunge through some bushes, skid around a boulder, and disappear. Furious, Benito pulled the boulder away. Felt the fox shoot past his body, and saw in the side of the hill a small, dark opening. Cautiously, he'd crawled inside. Found he wasn't in a den, but a tunnel, leading, it seemed, to the very heart of the hillside.

"Even to my sons I would confess I was truly afraid," Benito said. "It seemed to me like a pathway to Hell."

Concepción shivered and hastily made the sign of the cross. Benito nodded, then went on with his story.

Hell-bound or not, he hadn't given in to his fear. Lighting one match after another, he crawled along the bumpy, winding passage until finally, just when he began to wonder if he'd have enough matches to light his way out, he rounded a corner and found himself in a vaulted chamber where sunlight filtered down through a tangle of leaves and branches some twenty meters over his head.

"It was a pagan temple," he declared. "I know because right in the middle was the big stone slab where they sacrificed the virgins."

"Ay, Benito!"

"It's true. Remember what Father Juan told us about those pagans."

"You mean, told you and your friends."

"*Bueno,* that's as it should be," he said, and went on with his story.

He'd been heading back to the tunnel when he noticed a flight of steps hewn in one of the walls and leading to the skylight. Halfway up, he stopped and looked back. The afternoon sun was shining on one of the giant boulders that supported the slab.

"I thought I saw a niche," he said. "Some kind of hiding place."

Overcome by curiosity, he'd turned and gone back. Found the niche was sealed by a well-fitting stone. He'd tugged and pried, and finally the stone had fallen out and there was the box.

"And inside?" Concepción whispered.

Benito frowned. "You understand, you're not to talk about this with anyone."

Concepción touched the crucifix at her throat and nodded.

"And I alone decide what becomes of it."

She bit her lip. Nodded again.

Benito grunted and looked around. Andrés Rabal and two of his sons were striding toward the neighboring pasture, carrying scythes.

"Too late," he muttered, and picked up the box. "Come. I'll have to show you my treasure in the house."

## chapter 2

In the main room of the cottage, Concepción stood beside the table and watched her husband pull closed the heavy wooden shutters.

Who did he think was out there, she wondered. Unless he

was worried about the sky. Many people in Galicia were, imagining it to be filled with gods and demons from the pagan past. But Benito wasn't one of these. At least, he never used to be.

Nervously she fingered her silver crucifix, thinking right now it was hard to know exactly what Benito believed. Never had she seen him so excited. In fact, she was sure she'd sensed his animation in her sleep. That was what had jolted her out of her dream. Such a pleasant dream, too. She a girl of sixteen running barefoot beside a rushing river. Then wading into the current, leaping joyously from boulder to boulder . . .

Beside her, Benito lit a kerosene lamp. "Remember, not a word about this to anyone."

"Didn't I give you my solemn promise?"

She glanced at the Virgin, watching from the calendar. Would it be blasphemous, examining heathen treasure with Her looking on? Maybe the calendar should be turned to the wall. But what good would that do? The Virgin would still be there in spirit.

Benito lifted something out of the box and without a word placed it in her hands. She started. Looked down.

"Mother of God, Benito, what kind of—"

"Gold, *mujer*. Pure gold."

"Yes, but—"

"They could be worth a fortune."

"Who would buy a thing such as this?"

"The rich. The rich will buy anything."

Concepción sniffed, and turned the interlocked pair this way and that. Who could have made such a thing, she wondered. Certainly not a woman. No woman would ever think of doing it in that position. Yet their activity aside, she had to admit the figures were beautifully made. And the gold . . . it seemed almost to vibrate . . .

"They're not always like that," Benito said. "They come apart. Here, let me show you."

"No. I'm not through looking at them."

"Don't tell me you like them!"

She felt her face grow hot. "Ay, Benito. Give me a moment to think."

Suddenly she was overwhelmed by a memory. Herself at age ten, lying in a narrow cot, wondering what it would be like to see and touch the private places of a man. A ninety-degree angle, the girls at the convent school had said. And three times its normal size. Could such a thing be possible, she'd wondered. And had touched her own secret places, wondering where such a thing could possibly fit.

"Could a woman really receive it in that position?" she mused. "It would take years of practice. Almost, one might say, a vocation." She giggled. "Look, Benito. Look at her face. She's enjoying it as much as he is."

"Concepción, please. Control yourself."

"But look. She loves it. How is that possible?"

"How do I know? Here, let me—"

"They look so happy," she said, ignoring him. "As though what they're doing is the most natural thing in the world."

"Perhaps for them it was. You know what Father Juan told us."

"You, not me," she said automatically.

"So what's your decision?" Benito asked. "Do you like my treasure or don't you?"

She smiled.

"And what does that mean?"

"What do you think it means?"

"I don't believe it."

"It's the most indecent object I've ever seen," she said, her smile even broader.

Benito frowned. "What's wrong, *mujer*? I've never seen you like this."

"Does it frighten you?"

"Of course not."

"Me, too," she murmured, and moved toward him, thinking, strange, usually at a time like this she'd move away, avert her eyes. Why, she wondered. Shyness? Or something else, something she'd been taught by her mother and the nuns. They'd taught her so many things: how a woman should sit, stand, walk, listen. But not how to gaze in her husband's eyes. Such nice eyes, too. And such a nice face if you didn't mind the nose being too big, the mouth too wide, the ears . . .

"Woman, let go of my hand. And give me those statues."

She shook her head, studying the face that was, but seeing in her mind the face that used to be. Carefree, laughing. The face of a vibrant young man who one day had come striding up from the harbor when she, aged sixteen, was visiting her cousin Amalia. There they were, standing beside the fountain, laughing and chattering with Amalia's friends, and suddenly there he was, beret at an angle, asking for a drink of water.

She'd known him, of course. Everyone in Amor Milagroso knew one another. But this was the first time she'd stood so close, looked him full in the face. Then someone—his cousin Marta, perhaps—had said, "You remember Concepción Peralta." And Benito had grinned. Causing Concepción Peralta to turn away, afraid of the tingling below her belly, the sudden moistness between her legs.

"*Mujer*, what is it?" her husband demanded.

"Ay, Benito, Benito . . ."

Eyes wide, he pulled away his hand.

"Please," she breathed.

"You mean here? Now?"

She nodded.

"But—"

"Don't you want to?"

"Want to! Since I entered that cave I've felt like a youth of twenty."

"And I, right now, am like a girl of sixteen."

Setting the statues on the table, she pulled off her kerchief.

"Take me," she murmured, "take me . . ."

Eyes gentle, Benito put his arm around her waist and eased her to the cold stone floor.

Then take her he did, right there in the middle of the room, with the Virgin watching from the calendar and Concepción not caring, not caring at all.

# chapter 3 🌺🌺

While Benito and Concepción dallied on the cold stone floor, in the library of his villa Diego Granflaqueza y Fuerte Anhelo (duke of Última Alegría and direct descendant of Amor Milagroso's legendary founder) leaned his white head against the velvet of his chair and slipped a cigarette into a silver holder.

"So he's to leave from here," Don Diego said to the

brooding young man in the wing chair opposite him. "Frankly, I don't know whether to feel privileged or put upon."

"I'm sorry, your grace, but our group up in La Coruña is being watched."

"All of them?"

"Don't be alarmed, señor. I came the last ten kilometers on horseback through the woods."

"Ah . . . just as we used to do during the war."

"Yes. So I've heard . . ." The young man sighed and set down his sherry glass. "But to get back to our plans . . . for obvious reasons we've decided to use a fishing boat. Luckily there's one available right in this village. *La Mariposa.*"

"*The Butterfly.* Very appropriate."

"Not only that, she's been seen sailing in and out of this firth for years. Your grace sees the point."

"Of course."

"And he agrees?"

"I don't seem to have much choice."

"Nor do we, señor. That's why two of our men have already bid on the boat."

Don Diego glanced out the window. The sun was almost down, and the woods beyond the terrace were becoming shadowy.

"If anything goes wrong, can those men do what might become necessary?" he asked.

The younger man smiled. "During the war their parents were shot while Ramón and Pepe watched from the window. Believe me, your grace, those two have never forgotten."

The duke nodded and with half-closed eyes watched the smoke from his cigarette coil toward the ceiling. "From what you say," he murmured, "our mayor isn't going to enjoy this year's *Romería* at all."

"I hope that's no inconvenience."

The duke shrugged.

"It's by far the best time," the young man explained. "People wandering hither and yon. Nobody paying much attention."

"We hope."

"We hope." The young man picked up his attaché case. "Then it's agreed. Your grace will see *La Mariposa* becomes ours and nothing interferes with her internal modifications."

"You have my word," the duke replied. And rising from his chair, escorted his guest out to the terrace and wished him a safe journey back to La Coruña.


# chapter 4 🌸🌸


From somewhere out in the bay came the eerie moan of a conch shell.

Benito shivered and peered into the fog. He'd forgotten how cold it could be near the water early in the morning. But then he never used to wait patiently on the dock with the women; he used to be on one of the boats returning home. And thanks to his treasure, would be again . . .

*La Mariposa.* Not as fast as the *A Mi Gusto.* Or as spirited. But sturdy, dependable. Above all, available. No small thing along a coast where fishing boats passed from father to son. By heaven, Benito should have talked to Paco Camino yesterday. Would have except . . .

•

Who would have imagined Concepción insisting he bring the laughing lovers into the bedroom. Set them on the shelf above the foot of the bed.

"Now you light the candle," she said, "while I go pick us some flowers."

Benito shook his head in amazement. "Talk about pagan . . . it's a good thing María del Carmen is visiting her sister in Las Palomillas. Otherwise the poor girl would wonder what had become of us."

"And what has?" Concepción asked softly.

"I don't know," he murmured, pulling her gently onto the bed. "But for some reason I can't get enough of you."

"Nor I of you," she breathed.

Afterward, the candle unlit, the flowers unpicked, they lay side by side in the gathering twilight.

"Was it good for you, *mujer?*" he asked.

Concepción smiled. "I went up and up. Like one of those pink-and-white cherubs on the ceiling of the church."

"Imagine. Concepción Peralta de Bazán ascending to Heaven with her husband's—"

"Ay, Benito, enough." Laying her finger across his lips. "Such talk is wicked."

"Is it?" he asked. Then kissed her fingertips and moved her hand to his chest.

"I wonder," she mused, "do you suppose this treasure of yours is evil?"

"Of course not." Though secretly he wasn't so sure. Holy things never made him feel as good as this . . .

"You know what I wish?" Concepción said. "I wish with the money you get from your treasure we could bring Antonio home from Buenos Aires."

"If that is what the boy wants . . ."

"He does. I know it. And José could come home from Madrid. Live on the farm with his wife and children."

Benito frowned. "José isn't married."

"He will be. And so will Antonio. Oh, Benito, think. You'll be a grandfather."

"A twenty-year-old like me?" he laughed. "Impossible."

"What is your dream?" she asked shyly.

"My dream?" And staring at the shadowy ceiling, Benito at last told her that his greatest dream was to replace the *A Mi Gusto*. Go back to the sea and work side by side with their youngest son, Manolo.

"So you want to go back to being a fisherman," she whispered, as if the words stunned her.

"In truth, never have I felt at ease on your father's land."

That was when Concepción started crying. Not because they'd have to move back to the village, but because for five years her husband had been unhappy and only now had he had the courage to tell her so.

"Only now do I have the courage to do a lot of things," he said, and kissing away her tears, suggested she be courageous, too. "Please, at least once in your life, you be the one on top."

And she was. Not just once, but two, three . . .

An indignant sniff brought him back to the dock and the icy stare of the widow Mendoza. Puzzled, he nodded. Bade her a polite *buenos días*. Realizing only when she sniffed again and turned away that he must have been smiling and— horror of horrors—the widow Mendoza thought it was at her.

Cheeks burning, he pushed through the whispering crowd, feeling as though the women could read on his face all that had happened last night in his bed. Finally, standing on the end of the dock, he saw shadowy forms emerging from the mist. Keep calm, he told himself. Not much longer and the boats will be in, the fish sold, the women gone. Then when the boats were beached, the men spreading their nets, he'd saunter along the sand, say to Paco Camino . . .

"What do you mean *La Mariposa* might already be sold? Is she or isn't she?"

Without loosening his hold on the net, Paco Camino squinted at his friend through black-rimmed glasses, hazy with sea spray.

"She is and she isn't," he snapped.

"And what's that supposed to mean?"

"That I've received an offer but haven't yet accepted it."

"I see. And may a friend inquire what that offer was?"

Paco signaled his helpers to move farther down the beach, then with a sly grin whispered an amount three times higher than Benito had expected.

He whistled. "That's a lot of money, old man."

"That's a lot of boat, *amigo*."

Benito rubbed his hand along *La Mariposa*'s battered gunwale. She was a fine boat, all right. A good four-cylinder engine, watertight cabin, nets, floats, oars, anchor. Still, the price Paco had been offered was unbelievable.

"Who in Amor Milagroso has money like that?" he grumbled.

Paco chuckled. "Who said it was someone from Amor Milagroso?"

"You'd let *La Mariposa* be harbored somewhere else?"

"I didn't say that, either."

Benito heaved an impatient sigh. "All right, then. What did you say?"

"To the buyer?"

"Yes, to the buyer."

"No words at all."

With a raucous cackle the old fisherman waved good-bye to his crew, then as if sensing Benito's patience had been sorely tested, voluntarily added, "I talked to his go-betweens. Of course, I wasn't supposed to know that was what they were."

"But you did."

"*Claro.* Those two weren't fishermen. I could tell by their hands. Clean and soft. You know the kind of hands I mean, Benito."

"Somebody rich," he muttered. "But what does somebody rich want with a fishing boat?"

Paco shrugged. "All I know is they offered me a lot more money than I intended asking."

A wave of fatigue swept across Benito's body. It was always the same. The poor worked and dreamed while the rich took what they wanted and sailed away with it.

"So what did you tell them, these go-betweens?" he asked, eyes focused on a tiny crab sidling across the sand.

Paco grinned. "To come back here this morning. I told them I had to think about it. Which wasn't true, but oh, my friend, the pleasure I took in making them wait."

Benito nodded, then squared his shoulders. "I'll match their offer to the peseta."

"You, Benito? You?"

"Is someone else here?"

Paco moved closer, squinted up at Benito's face. "You're not well, my friend. I can see it in your eyes. They're feverish."

"Bah."

"No, truly. You have a strange look about you."

"Come on, *amigo*. Are you going to sell me that boat or aren't you?"

Paco frowned. "I don't know, Benito. I'm worried. Where are you going to get so much money?"

"I'll be able to pay you. Don't concern yourself about that."

Still studying Benito's face, the old man rubbed his hand across the stubble on his chin. "You haven't broken your vow, have you? Agreed to join that outlaw El Chavo?"

Benito started as once again he remembered the hoe. As soon as he left the beach, he'd head straight for the oak grove.

"You were here the morning after the storm," he said. "You heard what I pledged when Manolo despaired what would become of us."

Paco nodded toward his boat. "This is what Manolo should have—*La Mariposa*."

"Good God, isn't that what I'm saying?"

Paco grunted and climbed over the gunwale. "You know, of course, I need the money by the first of July."

"What! Why that's—when?—the middle of next week."

"Quiet!" Nodding at something farther down the beach. "Here comes Esteban What's-His-Name."

Benito glanced over his shoulder. Striding out of the mist was a stoop-shouldered man smoking a cigarette.

"The mayor's spies are out early this year," Benito muttered under his breath. Then, turning to the new arrival, shouted, "*Oye,* Esteban, how goes it?"

"So-so," Esteban replied, his narrowed eyes moving from Benito to Paco. "You sell your boat yet, old man?"

"Maybe. Maybe not," Paco announced, straightening the lines on the forward mast.

The stoop-shouldered man turned back to Benito. "We don't see you down here very often."

"True, true."

"Thinking of buying this boat yourself?"

"Who, me?" Benito laughed. "Where would I get the money to buy a fishing boat?"

"Where, indeed," Esteban said. Flipped away his cigarette, mumbled a curt *hasta luego,* and continued up the beach.

"This accursed village," Paco muttered, staring after him. "I'll be glad to get out of here."

"What's that?"

"Didn't I tell you? Because of the extra money, when my son and grandson move to Milan I'm going with them."

"So that's it." Knowing if the old man didn't leave with his family, he'd never have the courage to leave at all. But ten days . . .

"The go-betweens can pay me tomorrow," Paco announced, as though reading Benito's mind. "Naturally," he added, bending to a tangled mass of lines, floats, and extra clothing, "I'd rather the boat went to you and Manolo."

"Naturally," Benito said, then swallowed dryly. Ten days. He could go to Madrid, ask José to help him. It shouldn't take long to find a buyer. José worked in the Bureau of Social Security. He must meet thirty or forty rich *madrileños* every day . . .

He cleared his throat. "As I said before, I'll match their offer to the peseta."

Paco straightened up and for a few tense moments stared down at his friend as though considering his integrity as well as his offer. Then, cackling with delight, he thrust a claw-like hand over the gunwale.

"Agreed," he cried. "Ay, Benito, those men will be furious."

Suddenly Benito was painfully aware of Paco's weak eyes and frail body. "Listen, old man, when you tell them what you've done . . . take care, eh?"

"Look at me, *amigo*. Have I not fought the sea in all of her moods since I was fourteen years old? Can I not tell two men with soft hands I sold my boat to somebody else? If anyone should take care, Benito, it should be you."

"Bah. I'm not afraid. Yet now that I think about it . . . Yes. It would be better if you didn't tell them or anybody else who you sold to. I don't want everyone in the village wondering where Benito Bazán is getting so much money."

"But you can tell me, Benito. I'm your friend."

"The middle of next week," Benito said.

And set off for the village, deciding as he walked that since time was of the essence he'd go straight to the café and make the first long-distance call he'd ever made in his life.

# chapter 5

Ten in the morning and the fog still hadn't lifted. Pablo Estrada, for almost forty years mayor of Amor Milagroso, stood with his hands behind his back, contemplating the bleak gray world outside his window.

He was coming to despise the fog. It emphasized his feeling of being cut off, not just from the village and its people but from the rest of Spain and the winds of change that with the *Generalísimo*'s approaching death seemed ready to sweep across her plateaus and mountains.

The mayor sighed. Not much hope of sunshine today. The golden light that had warmed Amor Milagroso the first day of summer had been nothing but a fluke, a false promise things were getting better. The weather wasn't about to improve any more than the village itself.

At sixty-three, Pablo Estrada was getting tired of this town whose destiny he had come to control literally by accident. On that fateful day early in the war, Pablo, then in his twenties, was standing on the balcony of the city hall watching the then current mayor—his uncle Gregorio—exhort the villagers to support General Franco. Suddenly, in the middle of an exuberant gesture, Uncle Gregorio lost his balance and flipped over the railing onto his head.

That same afternoon, as though to deny the fatal accident had really happened, the villagers named Pablo his uncle's successor. The youth accepted on the spot, not only his uncle's post but his politics, coming in time to believe that the *Generalísimo* was destined not only to unify Spain but to make her the Christian leader of an increasingly pagan world. Then, in the last few months, Pablo Estrada had started changing his mind. Not liking the idea he was fallible, not wanting others to discover it as well, the mayor kept his growing disenchantment with the *Generalísimo* to himself. But he didn't feel good about the change in his loyalty. Any more than he felt good about the fog outside his window.

Turning from the glass, the mayor crossed to his desk,

settled himself in his chair, and smoothed the lapels of his pinstriped suit. Only then did he raise his eyes to the stoop-shouldered man waiting opposite him.

A familiar figure. Esteban Something-or-Other. The nephew of his late wife's cousin. Or maybe the cousin of his late wife's nephew. The mayor couldn't remember. They all looked and acted so much alike, these irregular employees. Eager to please, anxious to prove they had keen ears and sharp eyes and thus deserved higher pay, more important assignments. Perhaps, in time, promotion to the regular payroll. Where as dedicated civil servants they could close their eyes, stop up their ears, and be considered governmental assets.

"My clerk tells me you have news of two strangers," the mayor said.

"Yes, Don Pablo." The man kneaded his beret as though that were the source of his information.

"Well?" the mayor urged.

"They're pretending to be fishermen, Don Pablo. And yesterday afternoon they had a long talk with Paco Camino."

"Of what interest is that to me?" the mayor snapped. "Surely two strangers, no matter how they're dressed, can talk to a citizen without someone reporting the event to the mayor."

"Of course, Don Pablo, of course. I just thought at this particular time . . ."

His voice faded, but the mayor knew what Esteban was thinking. At this particular time everything unusual was to be reported at once. Those had been the mayor's own orders. Designed to make Amor Milagroso in the next thirty days the most moral, peaceful, law-abiding village on the coast. Why? So when Octavio Mora, arch-conservative and leader in the Cortes, climbed on the platform to deliver the opening address at this year's *Romería,* he'd be so impressed by Pablo

Estrada's administrative talents, he'd be overjoyed to recommend him for a more important post somewhere else.

The mayor drummed on his desk. "You say they talked with Paco Camino. Any idea what about?"

"His boat, Don Pablo. It's up for sale."

"You think El Chavo is thinking of adding to his fleet?"

"It's possible, Don Pablo."

"But not probable."

"No, Don Pablo."

The mayor leaned back and made a temple of his well-groomed fingers. Strangers asking about fishing boats . . . If they weren't smugglers, who were they?

"It may mean nothing, Don Pablo, but this morning Benito Bazán also spoke with Paco Camino."

"Did he, indeed?" The mayor tapped his templed fingers against his lips. Benito returning to the sea? Where could he be getting the money?

"I thought, Don Pablo, that since the Bazáns were—"

"I know, I know." Everyone knew the Bazáns had been Republicans. As had half the families in the village.

The mayor raised his hands and began a slow massage of his forehead. Not yet noon and already he was developing a headache. It was all so tiresome, this business of keeping the peace by paying one group to watch the other. Listening to reports. Trying to distinguish the real from the imagined, the significant from the trivial. And in the end, what did it matter? Neither group had a monopoly on either good or evil . . .

"That's it, then?" he asked.

"Yes, Don Pablo. Except that when he left the harbor, Benito went straight to the café. So far as I know, he's still there."

"Who's he waiting for?"

"I don't know, Don Pablo."

"Well, why didn't you— Oh, never mind."

The mayor rested his head in his hands. Strangers roaming the streets, citizens breaking their routines. And now, after all these years, were revolutionaries meeting again in the café? If so, what were they planning? A demonstration, perhaps. Against Octavio Mora . . .

Esteban cleared his throat. "If that's all, then, Don Pablo . . ."

The mayor reached for his billfold, aware, as he was so often, that the peace Amor Milagroso had enjoyed for over forty years hadn't come cheaply.

"You keep watch on Paco Camino," he said, handing some crumpled pesetas across the desk. "I'll assign someone else to watch Benito Bazán."

Deciding even as he spoke that Benito's guardian would be the Scarecrow, a man so lanky and awkward no one in the village took him seriously, much less suspected he was a spy.

The door closed, and the mayor looked at his watch. Half-past ten. A perfect time to enjoy something warm, and at the same time see what was happening in the café. Even if nothing was, he could gaze for a while at his fellow man instead of a dismal room and, beyond its windows, an unending vista of chill gray sky.

# chapter 6 🍀🍀

On most days at ten-thirty in the morning the café called *El Gran Gaitero,* or the Great Bagpipe Player (or the Big Windbag, as an American visitor once put it), a café named for its owner, Eliseo Rabal, the best piper in the village and the man who every year led the procession at the annual pilgrimage—not in the case of Amor Milagroso to the shrine of a local saint, but to the meadow beside the villa of Don Diego, one of the founding father's descendants—usually at that time of the morning the café was deserted, its early-morning coffee and *churro* customers long having gone about their business, its seafood and salad customers waiting for half-past twelve, which was the hour Eliseo started serving lunch. This morning, however, one of the tables in the rear of the wainscoted room had been occupied for three consecutive hours by Benito Bazán, who sat beside a half-filled bottle of wine (his second), staring first at the ancient telephone on the wall, then at the clock above the door to the central plaza.

Ten minus forty-three minutes. What was taking so long? Surely all the lines to Madrid couldn't be occupied. But then, hadn't the nephew of Roberto López made a *larga distancia* call only last year? And afterward, in this very room, hadn't he revealed what the operator had told him? That it wasn't the lines to Madrid one had to be concerned about. It was the two or three lines leading from Amor Milagroso. Lines so frayed, so fragile, that the weight of a raindrop could one day cause their collapse. Such a state of things. It was unbelievable, unbelievable . . .

Shaking his head, Benito poured himself another glass of wine. Wondering as he did so if the delay could possibly be in Madrid. Maybe the bureau where José worked had declared a holiday. Or José's superior had refused to let the call be put through. By heaven, it would be wonderful when the statues were sold and José could leave that miserable job. Come back where he belonged and work again in the open air. Though come to think of it, wasn't José the one who always used to get seasick? Of course. He was the one who most resembled the Peraltas.

Benito set down his glass and wondered again what his son was going to say when his father told him he was coming to Madrid, asked him to prepare a list of rich *madrileños*. Doubtless the boy would be overwhelmed. And wait until he saw those statues. His eyes would leap from their sockets while no doubt another part of his body . . . Benito chuckled, thinking it was a shame those laughing lovers had to be sold. Yet José didn't need them, and a man of fifty-five couldn't keep performing the way he was indefinitely.

Behind him the door to the central plaza opened and closed. Startled, Benito turned to see two men cross to a table near the window. They were dressed like fishermen—dark trousers, zipper jackets, berets—but even from across the room he could see their hands were soft and well cared for. Trying not to appear overly interested, Benito watched Eliseo clomp from the kitchen. Listened to the thinner of the two men order beer and a platter of prawns. If those were indeed the go-betweens, Benito thought, what had brought them to the café at this particular hour? A simple desire for food, perhaps. Or maybe Paco had forgotten his promise. If so, in a village like Amor Milagroso, it wouldn't take long to get Benito's description or learn he'd last been seen entering *El Gran Gaitero.*

Annoyed, Benito set down his glass. He didn't like the idea of being followed. Or having those men eavesdrop on his call to Madrid. Just as he was wondering whether or not he should cancel the call, the door opened again, and there stood Paco Camino.

Pushing up his glasses, the old man peered anxiously around the room, caught sight of the strangers, and made a beeline for the bar. A second later the door opened yet again, and in walked Esteban What's-His-Name. He, too, took one look around the room and headed straight for the bar, where he stood slumped in his jacket some fifteen meters from Paco Camino.

This is ridiculous, Benito thought. How could a man talk with his son about journeys and lists when listening to every word were the mayor's spy, a nosy friend, and two grim-faced strangers? There was no doubt in his mind now. He had to cancel that call immediately.

As if to taunt him, the telephone bell shrilled through the silence. Panicky, Benito pushed back his chair. Ran to the wall. Got there just as Eliseo reached around the door to the kitchen and lifted off the receiver.

"It's for you, Benito," he cried. "That *larga distancia* to your son in Madrid."

"I know who I'm calling," Benito muttered. And now, so did everybody else.

Scowling darkly, he grabbed the receiver from Eliseo's wet

hand, turned to the wall, and hunched over the mouthpiece.

"*Diga?*" he began softly.

Then louder: "*Sí*, José, it's me. Your father."

"Wrong? What could be wrong?"

Then louder still: "No, she's fine. Fine. In truth, she couldn't be better."

While José expressed his relief, Benito glanced back over his shoulder. One of the strangers was blowing his nose; the other was peeling a prawn. Meanwhile, across the room, Eliseo was serving Paco a cup of cocoa and Esteban was leaning against the bar, picking his teeth.

"What? No. The line is still open. I was just watching . . . never mind. Why I called, *mi hijo,* was to ask you . . . you see, I now own . . . *bueno,* let me put it this way . . ."

He wiped his brow and once again peered nervously over his shoulder. Inside the café nothing much had changed, but outside, approaching the door, was . . . Mother of God, Pablo Estrada, the mayor.

"Listen, José, I can't talk anymore."

"Yes, I know I haven't said anything. It's this village. People with nothing to do but—"

"No, of course I didn't call to tell you that. I called to—"

"Listen, José. You work in the Bureau of Social Security. Could you possibly . . ."

He swallowed, turned around. The mayor had entered the café and was now sitting in the middle of the room, watching Benito as though he were a program on television.

"What?" he shouted into the transmitter. "No, nothing's wrong with the equipment. It's all these people with—"

"Come home? Why should you— No, wait." Thinking there were other cities besides Madrid . . .

"Yes," he cried, "come home! We'll go to La Coruña. Santiago. Pontevedra!"

"How's that? Illness? Yes. Tell them it's illness. Your father." He chuckled, thinking of the laughing lovers. "Say if you don't go home, your father may never get out of bed."

# chapter 7

He couldn't believe his eyes. There were the bushes. There the slope from which he'd pulled away the rock. But no matter how much he swore, how often he pulled aside branches or scrabbled among leaves, that accursed hoe was nowhere to be found.

Tales of mutilated bodies discovered in the woods flashed across Benito's mind. He had to get out of there. Quick.

Heart pounding, he raced down the hill, through the vineyard, across the cabbage patch, and into the yard. Then made directly for the house and the kitchen, where Concepción sat near a window, mending a shirt.

"But you don't know for sure they've found it," she said when he'd finished his narration. "And even if they have, even if they come down to the farm and accuse you, you can always deny it."

"True," he agreed, and for a while felt better. Though later that afternoon as he guided the ox-drawn plow across the potato patch, he found he couldn't stop looking over his shoulder, jumping whenever a bird fluttered from a tree or a rabbit bounded out of the bushes.

Then, to make things worse, along about dusk he saw a flash of light on the hill before him. Puzzled, he stopped the oxen and stood perfectly still, scanning the greenery. Yes, there it was. A quick flash. Sunlight on glass. Someone was up there, watching him with binoculars. Should he run for cover, he wondered, or wait until they came down and got him?

Suddenly whoever was up there darted out from behind a tree, tripped on a log, and fell flat on his face. Benito sagged with relief. It wasn't the smugglers; it was the Scarecrow. Yet what was the mayor's stupidest spy doing here? Unless the mayor was afraid Benito was planning a revolution. With José called home to help with the paperwork . . .

Shaking his head, Benito watched the clumsy oaf get to his feet and take cover behind some bushes. Then he picked up his plow and continued down the furrow, noticing only when he reached the end of the field that Concepción was standing by the barn, waving at him frantically. He waved back, and immediately she pointed to two men striding toward him from the yard. Two men wearing black berets, zipper jackets, and dark trousers.

Benito's cheek throbbed with anger. It was just as he'd suspected. Paco had told them who he'd sold to, and now . . . what? They were coming to talk him out of it?

"Señores?" he said when at last they came within speaking distance.

"Forgive us for intruding," said the taller of the two, a balding man with high cheekbones and deep-set brown eyes. "I'm called Ramón Ramírez and this is my brother, Pepe."

Benito bowed. Mumbled his name. Asked how he could serve them.

"We saw you this morning down at the harbor," explained Pepe. More muscular than his brother, he was also—judging from his flushed cheeks and set lips—more easily irritated, if not downright surly. "Then when your friend told us he'd sold to somebody else," he went on, "we put two and two together and decided it must be you."

Benito smiled and spread wide his hands. "Alas, señores. Where would a farmer like me get the money to buy a fishing boat?"

"That was what we wondered, too," the balding man said, his brown eyes narrowed, "yet when we told the old man we knew for certain you were the buyer . . . well, let's just say he made no effort to convince us otherwise."

"You tricked him," Benito muttered.

"That's beside the point," said Ramón. "The point is you bought that boat and we want you to sell it to us."

"Bah. For what you offered, you could have any boat on this coast."

"That may be," Ramón conceded, "but we happen to want *La Mariposa*."

"I'm sorry. She's not for sale."

"Not even if we offered you a bonus?" Ramón asked softly.

Benito reached for his plow. "It's getting late, señores. If you'll excuse me . . ."

"Think it over, farmer," Pepe muttered. "My brother and I don't enjoy being disappointed."

"Nor do I, señores. *Buenas tardes*."

Ramón bowed. "We'll talk again tomorrow."

"A waste of your time and mine, Señor Ramírez."

"I doubt that," said Ramón. "You see, when Pepe gets angry, he gets a great deal more persuasive."

"And I a great deal more stubborn," Benito declared, and bidding them another curt good-bye, goaded the oxen and set off across the field, thinking if a man could live with spies and smugglers breathing down his neck, he could live with soft-handed go-betweens insisting he sell them a fishing boat. Besides, tomorrow José would be home. Or surely the day after.

# PART II 🍁🍁

# chapter 8

Five days after the frenzied telephone call from his father, José sat in the passenger seat of a Porsche, watching the wipers sweep aside the afternoon drizzle, wishing Don Miguel would change his mind, not insist on driving all the way to the farm.

Strange how a person's attitude could change in a couple of hours, José thought. In Santiago de Compostela it had seemed a lark, stepping out from amid the rain-soaked crowd waiting at the bus stop, climbing into this low white car whose bearded driver was obviously an aristocrat. And speeding along the highway it had been fun, exchanging information about people and places in Madrid. Speaking Castilian as though the two of them were native to that barren, windswept plateau instead of the moist green world outside the windows. Gradually, however, the well of small talk had run dry. Until now, careening through the hills above Amor Milagroso, José was coming to feel more and more aware of his windblown hair, his ill-fitting sports coat, his grandfather's battered suitcase. It had been one thing pretending equality with Miguel Granflaqueza on the open highway; it was quite another as the Porsche approached the turnoff to the farm.

Deciding he had to get out, had to put an end to this uncomfortable situation, José turned to the trim-bearded young noble, who by now was staring through the windshield with an air of bored detachment.

"Don Miguel," he began; then, calling forth the rhetorical skills seemingly inherent in every native of the Iberian Peninsula, told the nobleman how much he, José, had enjoyed riding in such a magnificent vehicle; how sorry he was that Don Miguel had been subjected to so much additional driving; then begged his grace to stop at the upcoming crossroad, from which it would be a simple matter for his passenger to proceed the rest of the way on foot.

"José, please," the nobleman sighed. "I told you before. I want to see what this car of mine can do."

"But your grace, that side road is nothing but—"

"Think of me as one of your neighbors. Or better yet"—putting a hand on José's thigh—"as one of your friends . . ."

José stiffened. "Your grace is very kind, but if the car could be stopped near that row of poplars . . ."

With a hearty laugh, Don Miguel put his hand back on the wheel and pressed his foot hard on the accelerator. The Porsche roared forward, skidded around the turn, clattered up the steep, stony track that led to the Peralta farm and a half-dozen others.

Angry, humiliated, José clung to the dashboard. What

right did this arrogant son of a duke have to ignore his request? Treat him like a potential playmate? Not that other men hadn't drawn the wrong conclusions from José's slight frame and delicate features, but my God, Don Miguel, a person he'd known from childhood. And today, when José was exhausted, out of his mind with worry. If the car weren't going so fast, he'd leap out and take his chances.

Just then he spotted, off to the left, the stone wall that marked the boundary of his grandfather's property. Then came the cornfield, the potato patch, the stone-legged Galician grain shed. His mind raced ahead to the house. Were they all right?

"There," he cried, pointing to a narrow driveway. "If your grace will stop near that . . ."

The following words died in his throat as Don Miguel spun the wheel and the Porsche splashed through a puddle, skidded around some chickens, and lurched to a stop under an apple tree. José sighed with relief, and hand on the latch, turned to say thank-you-and-good-bye, only to find himself staring not at Don Miguel's face but the back of his head.

Puzzled, José leaned forward. So far as he could tell, the nobleman was staring at a scrawny cow whose head and eyes were covered by a shaggy Galician rain hat. Now what was so intriguing about that, he wondered. Surely Don Miguel had seen a cow in a sheepskin rain hat before. Though never, perhaps, a cow as ancient as Engracia. It was a miracle the old girl was still alive and that those spindly legs were still able to support her.

"Don Miguel?"

"Hmmmmm?"

"If your grace will excuse me, I have to—"

"That hat. I must have that hat."

"Eh?"

"For my collection."

"Your grace collects cows' hats?"

The nobleman turned, and José was instantly reminded of the El Greco paintings he'd seen in the Prado. Portraits where everyone's features were a bit too long, and lurking about the eyes was a hint of madness.

"I collect folk art," Don Miguel announced. "I got interested when I was in college up at Cambridge, England. Besides . . ." He grinned wickedly. "That particular piece reminds me of the hat on a delightful guard outside of Buckingham Palace."

Feeling slightly dazed, José shook his head. "I don't know. I'll have to ask my—Oh God, my father! And my mother! Please. I have to leave now."

"No! Wait! What am I going to—"

But José was out of the car, running toward the house, the mud in the barnyard sucking at his patent-leather loafers. Ay, those wonderful new shoes. He'd saved for them for months; now here they were, being destroyed before his eyes. Anguished, he leaped to the concrete doorstep. Kicked them off. Then knocked on the door, and hearing no response, turned the handle and went in.

The house was silent, and for a moment José just stood there, staring at the open-beamed ceiling, the whitewashed walls, the simple wooden furniture. Strange to think he'd once called this place home. It seemed alien to him now, more alien than that day five years ago when he and his brothers had helped their parents move from the village. He remembered it had been difficult for his father to leave the fisherman's cottage where he and his sons had been born. Yet the farm would support them, while the sea—so long as Benito refused to work on another man's boat—no longer could. His mother, however, had been delighted to return to the Peralta land and the house she'd grown up in. He remembered she'd seemed almost eager to scrub once again the familiar stone floors, to polish the straight-backed chairs that stood by the great round table . . .

José started, suddenly aware of dusty surfaces, bedraggled flowers, an unwound clock. There was illness here, all right. His mother as well as his father.

Heart pounding, he turned toward the bedroom. The door was closed. Were they asleep? Bedridden? Anxiously he hurried forward. Raised his knuckles to the wood. Hesitated. What were those sounds? Deep breathing. Moans. My God, they were in pain. No, wait. That sounded almost as though . . . no. Impossible. Not his parents. Not so early in the afternoon.

He rapped on the wood. "*Papá*, it's me. José. I'm home to help you."

A grunt. Then his father's voice: "Who? What?"

"José. What's wrong, *papá*?"

Another grunt.

Then from behind him: "Please, señor. You're not supposed to disturb them. It's their rest period."

José caught his breath. That sweet voice. That Galician accent, like a melodious song, rising and falling.

He turned. Saw before him a wide-eyed girl with a basket of grapes on her arm. She was wearing a black kerchief, green sweater, plaid dress, and black rubber boots; looked about seventeen; and except for her scarlet cheeks, had the whitest skin José had ever seen.

"Who are you?" he gasped.

"María del Carmen Camino," she said, backing away from him.

María del Carmen. Of course. Three years ago. That letter from his brother Manolo saying María's mother had died, and Benito and Concepción were offering the girl a home. What else could they do? María surely couldn't live with her lecherous uncle Paco, and as for her married sisters and brothers, why, they were even poorer than the Bazáns. Besides, who could tell? Since Concepción had no living daughters and except for Manolo her sons had no wives, María's presence might prove a blessing.

"María del Carmen," murmured José, thinking, who would have thought such a skinny little nothing could develop into such a . . .

Eyes even wider, the girl backed away farther.

"No, wait," he cried. "Don't you remember me? I'm José."

"Ay, Don José." María del Carmen made the sign of the cross, her fingers touching one intriguing place after the other.

"No. Just José," he mumbled. Then raised his eyes. "My father sent for me. I had the feeling something was wrong."

"Something wrong?" a masculine voice called from the doorway. "Maybe I could be of help."

José looked over María's shoulder and saw Don Miguel leaning against the doorjamb, a mocking smile on his lips, José's battered suitcase at his feet.

"You didn't think I'd let you go without a decent good-bye," the nobleman cooed, "or without talking to your father about that beautiful rain hat."

"No, no, of course not. Please, your grace, come in."

"And what's this about trouble at the Casa Bazán?"

"Nothing, nothing."

"That's not what I've been hearing from my valet."

"Your valet's been talking about my parents?"

Don Miguel shrugged. "You know how it goes. The delivery boy tells the cook, the cook tells the . . . oh, no!"

Following the nobleman's lead, José looked down. Ringing Don Miguel's shoe was a clod of dung from which straws emerged like rays from a halo.

José gasped. Ran to the table and pulled out a chair. "Forgive me, your grace. I should have . . ." What? Swept the barnyard? Laid down a carpet? Nobody asked Don Miguel to get out of his car and look at Engracia's rain hat.

Cursing himself for ever having climbed into that Porsche, José watched María del Carmen drop to her knees and remove the nobleman's shoe, in the process offering him a magnificent view of her cleavage. José felt a pang of resentment. Why hadn't he been clever enough to step in a pile of cow dung?

"So my son is home at last," a voice boomed at his back, and José turned to see his father, the picture of health, striding forward to embrace him.

"What joy! What happiness!" Benito cried, folding him in a powerful *abrazo*. Then in José's ear: "Five days! What took you so long?"

"One doesn't leave his work without—"

Benito pushed back. "Now, then, *mi hijo*, let me look at you." Quickly his appraising eyes traveled from José's tousled hair to his checked sports coat, then down to his tight gray trousers and shoeless feet. Holy Mother of God, Benito's expression seemed to say, what has Madrid done to you?

Angered by his father's sharp words and silent criticism, José turned and gestured to the nobleman.

"Don Miguel saw me at the bus stop in Santiago," he said proudly. "He was testing his car and graciously brought me all the way to the farm."

"Don Miguel, this is truly an honor," Benito said. "I'm only sorry my wife isn't . . . oh, here she is."

He gestured to a dark-haired woman standing at the door to the bedroom in a pink satin blouse, flowered skirt, and rope-soled espadrilles.

"*Mamá*," croaked José, "what have you . . ."

She smiled, and as the door closed, José glimpsed on the bed embroidered sheets and a blue satin comforter.

"You look wonderful, *mi hijo*," said Concepción, and walked forward to enfold him in her strong, skinny arms. "Madrid seems to agree with you."

"And you," he gasped, pushing back for air, "you look, you look . . ."

"Unbelievable," Benito suggested. Then, putting an arm around her waist, guided her across the room to the seated nobleman.

José blinked. Never had he seen his father display so much affection. Not even when the family was alone, much less in the presence of a visitor.

"You remember Don Miguel," Benito said, as though the nobleman came to the farm often.

"Of course," she murmured, hand extended like a duchess.

"Señora Bazán." The nobleman rose quickly, and one shoe on, one shoe off, bent forward to kiss the knobby knuckles.

I don't believe this, José thought. Nor a minute or two later did he believe his father inviting Don Miguel into the living room.

"María del Carmen," Benito shouted when the nobleman accepted, "bring us that bottle of *albariño*. And you," he said, turning to José, "don't look so glum. This is a celebration."

"It is? For what event?"

"Has not the son of Don Diego honored us with a visit? And if that isn't enough, hasn't my own son come home from Madrid?"

"God knows why," José muttered.

"To be of service to his mother and father," Benito snapped, and flung wide the double doors that led to the living room.

Velvet drapes, flowered carpet, overstuffed furniture. No wonder he'd never liked this room, José thought. Everything in it had been picked out by his grandfather. Including that eyesore in the corner, a moldering dentist's chair the old man had found in some ruins and hauled to the farm, thinking when the war was over to sell it at a profit. As he hoped to do with the treadle sewing machine and the wind-up phonograph. But in the end, all Leopoldo Peralta's hard work and scheming got him was a bullet between the shoulder blades. The same as José's other grandfather. The only difference was that in the case of Leopoldo Peralta the assassin could have belonged to either side, while with Federico Bazán it was always clear the Republicans had his complete loyalty.

Restless, tired of hearing Don Miguel talk about Cambridge, José set down his wine and wandered over to the window. Outside, the sky was still gray, and over by the barn Engracia was still chewing her cud. Was it to see this he'd come all the way from the capital, he wondered. Canceled his plans for a vacation on the Costa Brava?

He turned from the window. Across the room Benito was telling Don Miguel how to put a nose ring in a pig. Suddenly José felt enraged. Trapped. Put upon. He had to get out of there. Now. Before he exploded.

"José, where are you going?" his mother called out as he approached the tall double doors.

"Air . . . I have to have air," he croaked. And before anyone could protest, he was in the other room, passing the kitchen, the table, the closed door to his parents' bedroom. Remembering the early siesta, the moans and grunts, he wondered again why his father had called him home, what was going on. And had he seen right? On that simple bed were there really embroidered sheets and a blue satin comforter? On impulse, he went back, opened the door, and looked.

Yes, there they were. His mother must have emptied her dowry chest. And what was on that shelf above the foot of the bed? Flowers. Candles. And something covered with a red velvet cloth.

Curious, José tiptoed into the room, raised his hand, and lifted a corner of the cloth. Then, puzzled by what he saw, pulled the cover off completely.

Mother of God, where had his parents found a thing like that? He lifted it down. The metal was as cold as ice, yet made his fingers tingle as though they were being charged with electricity. As for the effect of the interlocked male and female . . .

Openmouthed, José turned the golden lovers this way and that. They were fantastic, he thought. Truly fantastic. But could a woman really accept it in that position? María del Carmen, say. Could she bend over backward, spread those creamy white thighs . . .

At once he felt an urgent stirring in his tight gray trousers. Holy Mother of God, he had to get out of there. Hands shaking, he raised the statues to the shelf, only to freeze with horror as the woman slipped from the man and fell down onto the bed.

"Oh, no," he breathed. Picked her up, and still holding the man, tried to align organ and orifice. The lovers refused to cooperate. It was as though they were being perverse, laughing at him . . .

"Please," he moaned, "please . . ."

As if by magic, the figures clicked into position.

"Thank God," he sighed, and lifted them to the shelf.

"José, what are you doing?"

He wheeled. "*Mamá!*"

"You've found them," she cried. "Quick. Put them back before your father and—"

"Concepción, what are you doing in . . ." Benito froze, hand on the doorframe. "José. I thought you went— What are you— By heaven, is this what they teach you in Madrid? To sneak into people's rooms—"

"Shhhh, *papá*. Remember who's—"

"You tell me to be quiet! You!" Benito rushed forward. "To think a son of mine would spy on his own—"

"Benito, please." Concepción grabbed her husband by the forearm. "Don Miguel is right—"

"Anything wrong?" the nobleman asked from the doorway. "I thought I heard somebody mention 'spy.' Ah, José, it's you." His eyes moved to the interlocked statues. "And my, my, what's that?"

With an ingratiating smile, Benito backed Don Miguel out of the room. "Nothing, nothing. A small present for my wife's saint's day."

"That looks like real gold," said Don Miguel, backing up but still peering over Benito's shoulder.

"Real gold? Oh, no, your grace,"

"No?" Rump pressed against the edge of the table, the nobleman stopped and folded his arms. "That's interesting," he said, "because if it were, it would explain so much, wouldn't it? Why Benito Bazán made a long-distance call. Why his son came home. Why—"

"Coincidence, your grace. Nothing but coincidence."

"Perhaps. But the entire village is talking. . . . Fields untended. Lamps burning all night. People neglecting to go to Mass . . ."

"Neighbors with nothing to do but spy."

The nobleman picked some lint from his immaculate blue blazer. "I wonder . . . did you buy your wife's gift here in Amor Milagroso?"

"No. Yes. That is, no. I bought it somewhere else."

"Where, exactly?"

"Ah, señor, would that I could remember."

"Yes, it would be fortunate for you if you could."

"Fortunate, your grace?"

"Yes. Because, you see, the question is bound to arise: How did a statue that might be gold reach the bedroom of a Galician farmer?"

"Señor, are you suggesting—"

"I'm suggesting nothing. Merely asking the same question that will be put to you by the authorities."

Benito paled. "Your grace is going to discuss this matter with the authorities?"

"Isn't that the proper thing for a citizen in my position to do? Report a possible theft to his friend the mayor? Or perhaps another friend in the *Guardia Civil* . . ."

"The *Guardia*, yes." Benito wiped his brow with the sleeve of his work shirt.

"Such a citizen could, however, do something else," Don Miguel said softly. "He could find a buyer for that golden object. Provided, of course, the present owner agreed to look on him as a partner."

"I see. It's either your grace or the police."

"Precisely."

"It seems I have no choice," Benito said stiffly.

"No," the nobleman said with a smile, "I don't think you do."

# chapter 9

Exquisite, exquisite . . .

If the three of them weren't standing by the table, watching his every move, Don Miguel would be hard pressed not to clap his hands, jump up and down.

What a day this had been. First that delicious young boy over in Santiago. Then handsome José (though that seemed doomed, considering how he eyed that pudgy milkmaid). And now these scandalous, oh-so-golden statues. They made talking with those dreary, aging peasants worthwhile. Oh, my. To think there was a chance he could pay off those irksome debts, buy back that foolish letter to David. Maybe have enough for another car. Something between the Ferrari and the Porsche. A Jaguar, perhaps. In honor of those merry years in England.

Oh my, oh my, yes indeed. These statues were an absolute treasure. Celtic, he would guess, but as for their age he hadn't a clue. The Celts . . . did they come before the Vikings or after? Or were they one and the same? All he knew was that at one time one of them (or both if they were indeed synonymous) controlled almost the entire European continent, spreading as far east as . . . what was that below Russia? Asia Minor?

Oh, well. What mattered wasn't the history of the piece (an expert would know all about that) but its condition, the artistry with which it was made. Not to mention the subject matter. Too enchanting. Only what a pity it portrayed a man and a woman. Two men, that would have made it ambrosial. Yet even with such an obvious defect, hundreds, literally hundreds of people would be dying to buy it. The question was: Who could be trusted to do the selling?

Bobby? No. Too provincial. And too consumed by the eighteenth century.

Then how about Peter? Peter was a dear, but this farmer probably wasn't going to let the thing out of his sweaty hands. That meant Peter would have to come to Spain, and there'd be the tedious business of getting him a passport.

Which wouldn't, of course, be the case with Erik. Erik had more passports than he knew what to do with. A bit aloof (those Danes always were), but once you got him thawed out . . .

Don Miguel felt a pleasurable movement in his slim, checked trousers. He hadn't seen Erik since they were together at Cambridge, less than a year ago. They could make this a reunion, he thought. Combined with a vacation if the potential buyer lived in another country. Which he was almost certain to do. Who in Spain would invest in something like this? This treasure he could see in the collection of a sheik. Or of some grim-faced Oriental. He shivered. What fun it would be to get involved with another Japanese.

But in the meantime there was this lumpish farmer to deal with. Or was there? Once Erik arrived, there were ways. Don Miguel ought to know. Hadn't the Granflaquezas been using them for centuries?

# chapter 10

On the hillside behind the house, Benito propped his scythe against a tree, and shading his eyes from the afternoon sun, gazed down at the stony track that led to the Peralta farm and a half-dozen others.

Still no sign of the old fisherman. But he'd be there, never fear. Especially since José had told him the subject of the meeting would be money.

Mopping his brow, Benito moved to where he could look down on his family, wending their way homeward, the women with baskets of grass on their heads, José bent double from a bundle of grass on his back. How did the boy enjoy working in the fields after so many years sitting on his rump in Madrid, Benito wondered. And, more important, how did he like working side by side with the mother and father he'd forgotten how to honor? Imagine opening their bedroom door, walking in, pulling off that cloth. Well, it was too late to do anything about it now, but it would be a long time before Benito felt as close to the boy as he used to.

With a deep sigh he turned from the procession and

tramped back to the tree for yet another look at the distant roadway. Nothing had changed. No—wait. Two burros were angling across the lower pasture, one of them bearing Paco, the other . . .

"Manolo," he cried when the travelers finally crested the hill. "Why aren't you putting out to sea?"

"Paco told me you were in trouble," the young man replied, and dismounting from the burro, enfolded his father in a powerful *abrazo*.

"Ay, what a son," Benito breathed, tears welling in his eyes.

"That's why I'm here, too," Paco snapped. "Because I heard you were in trouble."

Benito released his son and turned to the old fisherman. "Is that what José told you?"

"José said you wanted to talk to me about money. Considering our agreement, if that doesn't mean trouble . . ."

Manolo frowned. "Agreement?"

"I'll explain later," Benito told him, and gestured to the shade beneath the tree. "Sit down, Paco, sit down," he urged. Then, in a whisper to his son: "*Oye*, Manolo. Sit on that rock and pretend to enjoy the view."

"Pretend?"

"Yes. You're the lookout."

"Fine, *papá*. But what am I looking for?"

"Spies. Smugglers. Strangers. Anybody."

Before Manolo could question him further, Benito hurried to the shade and sat down.

"So, Paco, you're here."

"Yes, Benito, I'm here. Though why we couldn't talk just as well in the café . . ."

"The walls in the café have ears," Benito declared.

"To hear what?"

"First, have some wine."

"Is the news that bad?"

"Bad? Who said anything about bad?"

"Then the news is good. We're going to celebrate. Ay, *amigo*! Can it be true? Is it today you're going to pay me?"

Benito waited until his friend had drunk deep from the goatskin flask before saying:

"My news is not bad, and it's not good. It's somewhere in the middle."

"Where, exactly, *amigo*?"

"Well, I'm still going to buy your boat."

"As we agreed."

"But you'll receive the money a little later than I planned. Say the tenth or eleventh of July."

"As we didn't agree. Benito, I told you. My son's buying my ticket the day after tomorrow."

"Tell him you'll pay him back."

"If my son had that kind of money, he wouldn't be moving to Milan in the first place. We're not all as rich as you are."

"I'm not rich, *amigo*. Otherwise, why would I be asking for extra time?"

"It's a hard world, Benito, a hard world."

For us, Benito thought, not for people like Don Miguel. People like Don Miguel invaded a man's house, seized his treasure, and announced they were going to sell it to a friend.

"Last night the go-betweens came again," Paco said softly.

"And?"

"They said if I would break my contract, they'd pay me the original price plus a bonus."

"Since you're so eager to leave, why didn't you do it?" Benito muttered.

"You're my friend, Benito. And we shook on it."

Benito reached for the *bota* and aimed a jet of liquid into his tight, parched throat.

"Don't worry, you'll be paid," he grumbled, wiping his lips. "I've found myself a treasure."

"A treasure!" Paco's glasses slid halfway down his nose. "What kind of treasure?"

Benito chuckled. "That's just what my wife asked."

"And what did you tell her?"

Benito waved a finger in front of his friend's face. "I told her it was a secret."

"Women can't keep secrets," Paco announced, picking up the wineskin.

"That's all right," Benito declared. "What's important, this morning I got a letter from Don— No, that's not important. What's important is an expert's going to buy my treasure the tenth of July."

"An expert in what?"

"If I told you, it wouldn't be a secret, would it?"

"No," Paco agreed. Then laid a hand on Benito's forearm. "But you can tell me where you found it, can't you?"

Benito shook his head. "Oh, no. Oh, no."

"Look, *papá*," Manolo called from the rock. "Are those the people I'm supposed to be watching for?"

Benito scrambled to his feet and hurried to the edge of the hill. In the distance below, some two dozen women in black were striding along the road, surrounded by at least a dozen running, skipping children. Benito frowned and rubbed the stubble on his chin. What was a procession of women and children doing on the road from Amor Milagroso?

"*Oye*, Manolo. Has anyone died lately?"

"*Por cierto, papá.*"

"I mean here. Along this road."

Manolo shrugged.

"No importance. That group consists of women and children. Since when is your father on guard against women and children?"

"Sometimes when my friends and I walk past the fountain," Manolo said, "the women drawing water look as though they could kill us."

"That's because their husbands haven't shown them who's boss," Paco called. *"Mujer en casa y la pata quebrada."*

"Times are changing, *hombre*," Benito said. "It would take more than a broken leg to keep them there these days."

Paco sniffed, and with as much dignity as he could muster, got to his feet, using the tree trunk for support.

"Time to go," he mumbled, and joining Benito on the edge of the hill, shaded his eyes and carefully scanned the lush green hillside. "Have to watch out for Esteban What's-His-Name," he mumbled. "Ever since that day on the beach, he's followed me everywhere."

"I got the Scarecrow," Benito announced.

"Why?" asked Manolo.

"The mayor's afraid Paco and I are going to blow up the world."

"Ay, Benito, look at that fog." The old man pointed toward the village, where wisps of gray could be seen drifting across the red-tiled roofs. "I never thought I'd say this, but you know, *amigo*, I'll be glad when my boat is sold and I can spend my nights walking with my son through the streets of Milan."

"Dodging whores and Fiats," Benito growled.

"Whores don't scare me," the old man chuckled. "And it's easier to dodge a Fiat than a cliff beneath the water." Then, apparently remembering the fate of the *A Mi Gusto*: "I'm sorry, *amigo*. It was the wine. I drank it too fast."

Benito nodded. "Then it's agreed," he said brusquely.

"What's agreed?"

"You'll arrive in Italy ten days after the others. I'll buy your ticket myself."

"I never agreed to that, Benito. We didn't even talk about it."

"So what does that mean? You're breaking our contract?"

"You're the one who's breaking our contract," Paco whined. "You said you'd have the money on the—"

"One week! That's all I'm asking."

"We're all going on the same train," Paco wailed. "My son says I can choose a seat that faces where I'm going or a seat that faces where I've been. I've already decided, Benito. I'm going to sit in a seat that faces forward."

"That's fine. You've got something to look forward to. But what about me?"

"There'll be another boat for sale someday."

"Ha!"

"And there's always the farm, Benito. It's very pretty up here. You can watch the fog without going out in it."

"So you'll sell to the go-betweens."

Paco rubbed his hands together nervously. "I need the money, *amigo*. I only hope they're still here."

"They haven't gone away. Not them. You want me to prove it?"

Cupping his palms around his mouth, Benito shouted to the hills and valleys:

"Hear ye, hear ye. *La Mariposa* is again for sale to the highest bidder."

Manolo ran to his father and grabbed him by the arm. *"Papá*, what are you doing?"

"Selling Paco's boat for him."

"Pablo Estrada will have you in jail for breaking the peace."

Benito shook himself free. "Pablo Estrada? What do I care for Pablo Estrada? Come on, Paco. You try. Call the go-betweens. Tell them you've changed your mind."

Paco backed away. "No, Benito, not that way. That way's crazy. I'll talk to them in the village."

"Why? And why settle for them? There may be more buyers in these hills than either of us realizes." Again he cupped his hands to his mouth. "*Oye, oye.* Last chance to buy the boat of Paco Camino."

Picking up the wineskin, he squeezed it dry, then sank to his knees and stared listlessly at the horizon.

"I'm going, Benito," Paco announced. "I'm sorry. I would have liked to . . ." Words failing, he reached out his hand.

"You'd better go, old man," Benito growled, turning away. "What if they run out of tickets?"

"*Papá*, please," Manolo urged. Then turned to the old fisherman: "Come on, Paco. I'll see you home."

"Don't forget to sit in the seat that faces forward," Benito shouted after them.

Manolo looked back over his shoulder. "Will you be all right?"

"Fine, fine. Even though I'll be sitting in a seat that faces nowhere."

"Start back to the farm, *papá*."

"I will, I will."

Face set, he watched his youngest son and Paco Camino start down the slope. Then, raising his eyes, gazed out at the blurry green hills, not sure if the moisture he felt on his cheeks came from tears or the advancing gray mist.

# chapter 11

Concepción pitched the last forkful of grass onto the pile beside the barn; then, wiping her brow, turned to her son, who together with María del Carmen was preparing to feed the pigs and the chickens.

"Listen, *mi hijo,* I may be overly concerned, but I'd prefer the two of you go back up the hill and keep watch over Benito."

"Both of us?" José sounded surprised.

Concepción smiled. "I thought María might like to hear about Madrid. Unless, of course, she's too tired. What do you say, María? Do you want to walk all that way or not?"

Eyes on her boots, María nodded.

"Then be off with you," Concepción said. "And hurry. Even if Paco arrives, he won't stay with Benito forever."

José agreed, and the young folks set off for the hillside.

Concepción watched them go, wondering if she'd done the right thing, tempting fate, maybe compromising the girl's honor. Yet if a mother couldn't trust her own flesh and blood . . . And María del Carmen needed experience talking with a man her own age.

Absent-mindedly, Concepción patted the cow's forehead. Poor old Engracia. How naked she looked without her sheepskin rain hat. Still, Don Miguel had given them a good price. It made one wonder if there were other things on the farm that could be sold as folk art. Yet how did one know what was art and what only rubbish?

Walking to the cottage, Concepción raised her eyes to José and María, now halfway up the steep green slope. Ay, what a handsome couple, she thought. He so slender and straight, she so demure and graceful—even in those flopping rubber boots. Poor María del Carmen. She'd marry, of course. And afterward would come the births and the deaths, the endless toil. But there would be joy, too. And when the flame of life began to flicker, grandchildren would arrive and illuminate the darkness.

As she kicked off her wooden shoes, Concepción felt a sudden pang of sadness. Surely there must be another path a girl like María del Carmen could follow, but what it was and where it might lead, Concepción couldn't begin to imagine. María might find out, though. Things—the world—seemed to be changing.

Hand on the latch, Concepción glanced again at the hillside, but the couple had either crested the rise or struck off on the alternate path through the woodland. She felt another pang of conscience. Her own mother never would have allowed José and María so much freedom. Nor would Concepción herself, a week ago.

Something in me has changed, too, she thought, entering the shadowy farmhouse. What, she didn't know, but it seemed wrong to insist José and María follow the same path she and Benito had. They should have a chance to strike out on their own. But oh, dear God, what if the route they chose brought them nothing but heartache?

Disturbed by this unfamiliar chain of thoughts, Concepción wandered aimlessly around the room, moving a chair here, straightening a doily there. Then, on the way to the bedroom, she stopped to gaze in wonder at a black-framed photograph. There sat Benito in the black suit he still wore to weddings and funerals. And there, her slender hand resting lightly on his shoulder, stood a young woman in a black dress and black mantilla. Was that really Concepción at age twenty? That somber señorita dressed for mourning? She remembered she'd wanted to break with tradition, be married in white, but her mother said no. Of what use was a white dress in a village where occasions of joy were far outnumbered by occasions of sorrow?

Concepción raised work-worn fingers to her coarse, dry cheek. A better way . . . Was it possible there was a better way?

Sadder than ever, she went into the bedroom and on impulse pulled the cloth from the statues above the bed. There they were, united in joy. As she and Benito were united. But only now. Only after thirty long years. Why had no one told them of the communion possible between a man and a woman? Could it be, no one in the village knew?

Suddenly, staring at the laughing lovers, Concepción remembered Benito's request that she reveal herself to him naked. She who barely took off her clothes to wash. Yet perhaps if she got used to it . . . Perhaps if she prepared herself in advance . . .

She bit her lip. Should she? It would be indecent, lying naked beneath the covers, waiting for her husband to return from the upper pasture. But what pleasure she would bring him, what proof she was willing to rid herself of old customs, old fears . . .

With trembling fingers she unbuttoned the neck of her plaid dress. Then reached under the skirt and unrolled the tops of her black cotton stockings. Pulled them off. Threw them into the wardrobe, to be followed, seconds later, by her white cotton pants. Then it was off with the dress, off with the slip, and there she stood: stark naked except for her crucifix. That seemed sacrilegious, so she took it off and hung it on a hook. Shivering with cold and excitement, she hurried to the bed and pulled back the blue satin comforter. Hesitated, one knee on the mattress. No, she couldn't be a coward. She had to do it. She had to look at herself.

Heart pounding, she padded to the mirror and stared at her reflection. Not just at the gaunt face with its burning cheeks and frenzied eyes, but at the lean neck, the bony shoulders, the small breasts beginning to sag, the . . .

What was that noise?

At once she stiffened, cocked an ear to the door. Somebody was outside the house, pounding to get in.

"Concepción!"

A woman's voice, loud and demanding.

Concepción darted to the wardrobe. Was reaching for her pants when someone tapped on the window beside her. She wheeled, saw a dark form through the chinks in the shutters. Somebody was being lifted to the window by somebody else. But who?

Blindly she reached inside the wardrobe. Pulled out the first thing she touched. A green satin dress she'd inherited years ago from her cousin Amalia.

"Concepción!"

The voice was louder now, the pounding more insistent.

Concepción hurried from the bedroom, slamming the door behind her. "I'm coming, I'm coming," she called, buttoning her dress as she ran.

At the door she paused, wondering if she should look for a

weapon. But what? A vase? A nearby umbrella? Ridiculous. That wasn't a smuggler out there, or one of the strangers. It was a woman, probably with a couple of mischievous children trying to see in the bedroom window.

Taking a deep breath, she pulled open the door. There stood not one woman but fifteen or twenty. All of them dressed in black, most of them carrying baskets.

Concepción's hand flew to her chest, discovered not a cross but a misbuttoned dress. Quickly she clutched at the resulting gap, wondering if anyone had glimpsed her naked breasts.

"*Buenas tardes,* Concepción." Isabel García's pudgy face was a study in disapproval.

"Don't be afraid," murmured Victoria Montalvo, a widow for twenty-eight years, but always gentle and uncomplaining.

"That's enough, Victoria," snapped Teresa León, whose sharp tongue and fiery eyes were a village legend. "Remember, Isabel is to do all the talking."

Victoria nodded, and Isabel promptly filled her ample chest with air. "We came to discuss something serious, Concepción, but it appears—"

"Don't just stand there!" a cackling voice interrupted. "Look in her eyes. Look in her eyes."

Concepción turned. Saw rounding the corner of the house a shriveled old crone, followed by half a dozen nuns in their long black habits.

"Tía Rosa," she gasped, and searched again for the missing crucifix. Everyone knew Tía Rosa was a witch . . .

"Teresa thought her powers might be useful," Victoria said softly.

"And I agreed," said Isabel. "Provided Father Juan came along, too."

"Father Juan," Concepción croaked. "You've brought Father Juan?"

Isabel smiled triumphantly. "He's right over there."

And indeed he was. Standing with his back to the group, watching a dozen or so young children playing beneath the apple tree.

Concepción panicked. What would Father Juan think when he saw her bare feet, her bare legs . . . and ay, *por Dios,* what if he, what if any of them, were to catch sight of those golden statues?

"Concepción, you're not paying attention," Isabel said peevishly. "As I said before, we've come here to discuss something important."

"Not realizing we'd be interrupting your siesta," cooed Belita Sánchez, a recent bride but already five months pregnant.

"She should be up, anyway," Teresa snapped. "It's four o'clock, at least. She should be tending to the animals."

"From that dress and the look in her eyes, I'd say she was about to tend to something else," Belita giggled.

"Her eyes. Her eyes," cried Tía Rosa, pushing into the group. "Let me in so I can look at her eyes."

"In a moment, Tía Rosa," Isabel said primly. "First I have to explain why we're here."

"Then do it," Concepción demanded.

Teresa drew herself up. "We're here because things have been noticed."

"Things?"

"Lamps burning all night. People forgetting to go to Mass. People humming in the market."

"But that's ridiculous," Concepción protested. "Just because things are different, what right do you have to accuse a person of . . . of . . ."

"Of what?" asked Isabel. "So far we haven't accused anyone of anything."

"Now, now," said Father Juan, coming up behind Isabel's shoulder. "We mustn't forget we're here to help our afflicted sister, not condemn her."

"Let me in," yelped Tía Rosa, and burst through to the inner circle. "There. That's better. Now I can see what's happening behind those eyes."

"No," cried Concepción. And took an instinctive step backward.

Teresa moved closer. "Tía Rosa's right. We have to see what we can see."

"Yes. It has to be done," Isabel agreed.

Concepción thrust out her hands and backed away. "No. Stay back. Wait. Stop. Let me be."

"Oh, dear," moaned Victoria Montalvo as the group surged forward. "I don't like this at all."

"Stay back. Stay back," wailed Concepción, and rump pressed against the table, spied Tía Rosa hobbling toward the door to the bedroom.

"There are powers at work here," the old crone cackled. "I know. I can feel them."

"Tía Rosa. No!" Concepción shouted, and lunged forward, only to have Teresa and Isabel grab her by the arms.

"Those eyes look feverish," said Isabel.

"And look at those cheeks," said Teresa.

"Stop it. Let me go!" Concepción twisted her body and strained to free herself.

"Don't be afraid," Victoria murmured. "We only want to help."

"And Father Juan says it doesn't hurt much at all," Belita Sánchez added.

Fear galloped down Concepción's backbone. "What doesn't?"

"You'll see," Teresa snapped.

Isabel drew herself up to a proud five-foot-three. "Father Juan also says it's more common than we think."

"And sometimes takes a long time to cure," Belita put in. "That's why we brought the food baskets."

Across the room, Tía Rosa rattled the bedroom doorknob. "This is the place. I can smell them. They're right behind this door."

"No! Don't go in there," Concepción called out, but it was already too late. The door was open, and the old crone was entering the room, Father Juan and the nuns right behind her.

Teresa nudged Isabel in the ribs. "It's a good thing we came. Look at her expression."

"*Mi madre,* it's true." Isabel made the sign of the cross, in her confusion tapping Victoria's shoulder instead of her own. "Oh, Concepción, Concepción," she wailed.

Belita Sánchez picked up the refrain. "Ay, *mi madre, mi madre . . .*"

"Let me go!" Concepción shouted, and with the strength born of desperation, broke loose from her captors, darted to the wall, and lifted down a big black umbrella. Using its point like the tip of a sword, she charged into the crowded bedroom.

"Out!" she hollered. "All of you. Out of this room. Out of this house. Now."

Standing on the bed, Tía Rosa waved the interlocked statues like a trophy. "See, see," she croaked. "I told you. I told you."

"By heaven, what does a woman have to do?" Blind with

rage, Concepción rammed the tip of her umbrella into the nearest black buttock.

At once a pudgy hand reached back and removed the offending piece of metal. "Please, daughter. That's very uncomfortable."

Concepción's mouth sagged along with her weapon. "Father Juan . . . I didn't . . ."

"We'll talk about that later," he said. "Here, Tía Rosa. Give that to me."

Concepción leaned against the doorjamb, aware more and more women were crowding into the bedroom. No use struggling. It was all over. Father Juan would take the treasure, and Benito would kill her.

"Look. Look. They come apart," shrieked Tía Rosa, jumping up and down on the mattress.

"Please, my daughter," said Father Juan. "Those figures may be very valuable. Give them to me before—"

"And they go together again, too," she chortled. "Look, everybody. In. Out. In. Out."

"Oh, my God," a woman wailed. "Stop it."

"Here. Give them to me." Reaching around the priest, Teresa pulled the statues from the old woman's hand and started elbowing her way out of the bedroom.

"Bring them out here," Belita called from the other room.

"No," said Father Juan. "Really, señoras, I must insist. This is most—"

"Don't push, don't push," Teresa grumbled to the women around her. Then raised her hand. "Here, Isabel. You take them."

"Ooohh," the pudgy woman gasped, "they feel so . . . and oh . . ." Pulling the figures apart. "Look at that little fellow's—"

"Señoras. Please." Father Juan came striding out of the bedroom. "Are you Christian wives and mothers or a group of—"

"Here, Isabel. Over here."

"Then to me."

"Then me."

"Señoras, I command you to—"

"*Un momento!*" Brandishing the umbrella like a club, Concepción moved at last out of the doorway. "Give them to me," she cried. "Those statues belong to me."

"Very interesting," said Father Juan. "And where exactly did you get them, Señora Bazán?"

"That is of no concern to anyone," she retorted, and striding across the room, grabbed the figures from the hands of the widow Mendoza.

"Well, my daughters, that seems to be that." The priest smoothed back his hair and adjusted his collar. "However, before we depart, if the Señora Bazán would be so gracious . . . her priest and confessor would like a closer look at those remarkable objects."

Concepción hesitated, then meekly handed him the statues. What else could she do? Besides, now that their existence was no longer a secret, it was only a matter of time before someone took them from her forever.

"Quite lovely," murmured the priest, turning the separated pieces this way and that. "Oh, yes, quite lovely. Celtic, I should think. Quite possibly the god Lugus entering his personal source of power. And very ancient, too. I'd say six hundred years before the birth of our Lord."

His smile faded as he handed the statues back to Concepción. "Nevertheless, this is hardly what one would expect to find in a Christian bedroom, Señora Bazán. And then there's the question of where they came from." He sighed. "I'm sorry, my daughter, but I'm afraid I'll have to discuss this entire matter with our beloved mayor, Pablo Estrada."

# chapter 12 🌸🌸🌸

They had topped the first rise, and before them loomed a grassy slope dotted with dandelions.

José shaded his eyes. "What do you say, María? Shall we go straight up the slope or angle through the woods?"

Her eyes widened. "The woods?"

"I thought it might be cooler."

"Oh. Yes, I suppose it would."

"Then it's agreed."

With a cheery grin, José struck off toward the trees while in her clumsy boots María struggled to keep up with him.

He liked watching her make that effort. Liked the way she stretched out her long, thin legs. Swung her arms, forcing one breast and then the other against the thin cotton of her dress. As part of him was pushing against the cotton of his shorts. And had been, more in the past twenty-four hours than ever before in his life.

Because of the statues, he'd decided the night before, when, arguments and explanations over, he'd lain on his cot thinking about the backbending woman as his rod grew sturdy as a post. Again and again. Each time her image flashed across his mind. As it was now . . .

I've got to control myself, he thought, and a breathtaking possibility invaded his consciousness: What if María had seen and touched those statues, too?

He cleared his throat. "María?"

"Sí?"

"I was wondering . . . did you ever . . . that is, does my mother seem different to you lately?"

"You mean her clothes?"

"And other things."

"She smiles more."

"Aha. Any idea why?"

María blushed and turned away.

And what did that mean, he wondered. That she'd never tiptoed into that room, or that she had but was ashamed to admit it?

"Your father's different, too," she volunteered. "He's much more friendly. Even to a hired girl like me."

I can imagine, thought José, forcing his eyes away from her bustline. "Yes, but why?" he persisted.

"Maybe because he likes me."

"Of course he likes you! Who wouldn't? That's not the—"

"Oh, look, José! A chipmunk!"

José watched the little beast scurry along a branch, wondering what María would do if he ordered her to strip naked, bend slowly back so he could—

"José?"

"Hmmmmm?"

"In Madrid . . . when you go to that big park you told us about last night, do you . . . do you go there with a girl?"

72

"Sometimes," he lied. "City girls go anywhere they want."

"They do?"

Oh, God. Those eyes . . .

"You look tired," he said. "Here. Let's sit on this log a minute."

María caught her breath. "I don't know. Maybe we should . . ."

"Come on," he urged. Sat down and lit up a cigarette. "Nobody's going to hurt you."

"I know," she whispered. Then joined him on the log and tucked her skirt primly around her knees. "It's nice here," she ventured after a moment.

"If you enjoy being where nothing is going on." He breathed out a cloud of smoke, watched it merge with the breeze and disappear.

"Where you live, things must be happening all the time," she suggested.

"That's right, they are."

"Could you . . . would you tell me about it?"

"If you like," he said, and reminding himself his mother trusted him to keep his hands to himself, told her about life in the district near the Plaza Mayor. Feeling as he talked like a sophisticated man of the world. So on he went. Described the bullring, the Prado, the wonders he'd seen on his bus ride to Santiago.

"And the girls?" María breathed when he finished. "Are they prettier in other parts of Spain than they are here?"

His mouth dropped. Was that all she was interested in? How pretty she was?

"José, what is it? Have I said something wrong?"

"No. Your conversation is wonderful."

Then noticed her eyes were moist, her lips trembling. Oh, God, now she's going to cry, he thought. And then what? He'd put his arm around her shoulders. Kiss her on the eyes, the cheek, the . . .

"José, please. What is it?"

"Oh, God," he groaned. "Quick. Let's get out of here."

"You're right," she cried, springing to her feet. "If we're not careful, Uncle Paco's going to leave and your father's going to be on that hilltop alone."

# chapter 13

The sun had been obscured by the fog, but under the tree Benito still sat, unmoving. What difference did it make if he sat there forever? What difference did anything make now that *La Mariposa* was being sold to the go-betweens?

Leaning against the trunk, Benito watched tendrils of mist drifting across the lower pasture. Soon they would advance up the hill, wrap him and his tree in a chill gray shroud. What difference did that make, either? Since he'd lost all chance of being buried in the fog at sea, he might as well be buried in the fog on land. With no one to bid him farewell. Not his wife. Not his sons. Not his friends. Nobody.

A twig snapped in the bushes behind him. Startled, he turned around. Mother of God. The go-betweens hadn't run down the hill after Paco; they were marching toward him out of the shrubbery.

He scrambled to his feet. "*Oye,* señores, didn't I tell you yesterday that if you trespassed one more time—"

"Today's the day, farmer," Pepe snarled. "Either you sell us that boat or you tell us who's paying you to keep it away from us."

"Ridiculous. Nobody's paying me to do anything. Now get off this land before—"

"So nobody's paying you," the balding Ramón said softly. "Isn't that interesting? That means you can sell us that boat on your own."

"You're crazy. Didn't you hear me shouting? Paco's selling that boat, not me."

"Did you hear that?" Ramón asked his brother.

"I heard nothing," Pepe answered, "except that this fool refuses to cooperate."

"That's what I heard, too," Ramón agreed, "so let's go to it."

Pepe lunged. Grabbed Benito's arm and wrenched it upward behind his back.

"Who's paying you?" Ramón demanded.

"Aieeeeee!!!! Nobody!" Benito shrieked, and swung wildly with his other hand. Only to have that hand seized by Ramón, who, shouting to his brother to let go, flipped Benito over onto his back.

Fearful his spine had been crushed, Benito lay amid the leaves, gasping for breath. At once the brothers moved in, and one on either side, began kicking him with their sturdy work shoes.

"No! Stop!" Benito hollered, rolling onto his side. "Wait. You're making a mistake."

"You're the one who made the mistake," Pepe cried. "You made us lose an entire week."

"No, I didn't. Wait. Stop!"

But on they went, aiming their kicks at his shoulders, head, stomach, knees, kidneys . . .

"No, no," Benito groaned, shielding himself as best he could by curling into a ball and putting his arms over his head.

"You lied," Pepe snarled, drawing a knife. "You're working for them. Admit it."

"No!" Benito shrieked. "No. Wait. I beg you."

Pepe laughed. "Say your prayers, farmer. On this day you join your—"

"Stop!" a male voice commanded. "My pistol is aimed directly at your forehead."

"Run!" Ramón yelled, and the brothers darted across the grass, raced down the slope, and disappeared into the mist.

Benito moaned. Rolled over. Opened an eye.

Rubber boots were running toward him. Above were spindly legs, an ancient sweater, a skull-like face, tousled hair . . .

The boots tripped on a rock.

"Scarecrow," Benito breathed.

"Pablo told me never to reveal myself," the man panted, "but I couldn't let them kill you, Benito, could I?"

"You could," Benito gasped, "but you didn't. Thanks, *amigo*."

"*De nada*, Benito, but I almost didn't get here. When I heard you shouting, I was down in the glen finishing some cheese and pigs' feet."

Benito moaned and rolled onto his back.

"Are you hurt bad, *hermano*?" the Scarecrow asked.

"Bad enough."

"Take heart. Your son José and the niece of Paco Camino are even now appearing over the—"

"Paco!" Eyes wild, Benito sat up. "We've got to help him. That's where they're going."

"*Sí*, Benito, *sí*. But first we have to help you."

Benito sighed and closed his burning eyes, wondering as he sank into dreamy grayness why of all the people who might have saved his life it had to be a spy of Pablo Estrada the mayor.

# chapter 14

"What was that thump?"

Benito tried to sit up, groaned, fell back on the embroidered pillow.

"The wind," answered Concepción, and pulled up the comforter so it nestled around his chin.

"The wind doesn't thump. Things thump. People thump."

"Maybe it was José," she sighed. "Maybe he went outside to relieve himself."

"Light the candle."

"*Oye,* Benito, there's nothing—"

"I may be in pain, but I still command here. Light the candle."

Muttering under her breath, Concepción crawled out of bed and did as she was told.

"Did you really prod Father Juan with an umbrella?" Benito asked as he gazed at the shelf above their bed where the candle now cast a flickering light on the golden twosome. "He must have thought you were the Devil himself. No, herself."

"Shhhhh. Try to rest."

"I can't. One of them kicked my bad knee."

"I know. I saw. It's swollen."

"Imagine being rescued by a spy of the mayor," Benito grumbled.

"Try not to move around so much."

"We haven't heard the last of this," Benito said. "He won't forget, you know."

"Who? The Scarecrow? Or Pablo Estrada?"

"No, Father Juan."

"What do you think he'll do?" she asked, biting her lip.

"Who knows. Talk to the mayor. The police. Tell them Señora Bazán assaulted a man of the cloth. That she has in her house stolen property."

"That statue isn't— I mean, it isn't as though you deliberately— Benito? Are you listening?"

"Yes. And I heard it again."

"Wait here," Concepción cried, and flinging back the covers, leaped out of bed, grabbed the candle, and ran from the room.

"Over here, *mamá*," José whispered in the darkness. "Somebody hammered on the door. I'm going to see who it is."

"No, *mi hijo*, no!"

"What are we going to do? Cringe here all night?"

"If we have to."

"What's going on?" Benito called from the bedroom doorway.

"Ay, *mi madre*," Concepción cried, and taking one look at his wobbly legs encased in summer-weight gray underwear, set the candle on the table, rushed to his side, and put an arm around his waist to support him.

"Let me be," he protested. "Am I not man enough to—"

"*Sí, hombre*," she gasped as he sagged against her, "you're man enough for anything, but not right at the moment."

A short time later, Benito in bed, she came back to the main room, to find José had lit a lamp and María del Carmen come down from the loft clad in a cotton nightgown.

"It's been quiet for five minutes," José announced. "I'm going to open the door and look."

"No," Concepción cried, "they may be waiting out there with guns."

"Who?" asked María del Carmen.

"God knows," Concepción said, and as José cautiously opened the door, reached for her crucifix.

"Silent as a graveyard," he whispered, and stuck his head out farther. "Not a soul in— Wait. What's this?"

"I don't know," his mother moaned, "what?"

"A letter, nailed to the door."

He pulled loose a single typewritten sheet, brought it inside, and closed the door.

"Who's it from?" Concepción demanded.

José squinted at the signature. "Hard to tell, but I think it's El Chavo."

"A threat!"

"No. More like a business letter."

"Read it, *mi hijo*, read it."

José cleared his throat. " 'My dear Benito. Recently, on my return from La Coruña, my colleagues informed me a trespasser had entered my private warehouse and left behind him a hoe. This hoe has now been identified as yours.' "

"Ay, señora," María wailed. "I forgot to tell you. The other day when I was weeding the turnips—"

"I know. A man approached you with a hoe," Concepción said flatly.

María nodded. "He said he'd found it beside the road and wondered who it belonged to. So I looked and there were the nicks I myself had made by working too near the wall of the vineyard."

Concepción shook her head sadly. "I should have warned you . . ."

"He wants to see him," José reported. "Listen: 'This hoe, together with an empty niche, together with gossip heard in the market, leads me to believe something of value has been removed from my property. Please, tomorrow morning, come to the aforementioned warehouse to discuss this. Otherwise, as is usual in my organization, the matter will be resolved by my associate.' "

"El Bruto!" María gasped.

"That maniac," José said fiercely. "Why hasn't somebody put a stop to him?"

"Who?" Concepción snapped. "The men he's murdered? Their widows? Me?"

"No, of course not. Somebody who could—"

"Wait a minute. Why not me?"

"*Mamá,* you're a woman."

"Does that mean I'm not a citizen? Not afraid of what that madman's going to do next?"

"Please, *mamá.* Sit down. Calm yourself."

"I'm serious, *mi hijo.* If things have to change, why can't women take action, too?"

"What's come over you?" José asked. "You sound like one of those Italian women I saw on television. They want to change things. They want the right to have abortions."

"*Mi madre,*" Concepción gasped, and crossed herself quickly. Then with a frown:

"Yet if things are truly to change . . ."

"*Mamá,* it's way after midnight. We've got to decide— Wait! What's that?"

"More pounding," she exclaimed. "Quick. Get your grandfather's gun. It's in the—"

"*Papá,* hurry," a voice called from outside. "It's me. Manolo. I've got Paco Camino out here on a cart."

José pulled open the door as Concepción and María rushed up behind him.

"Something's wrong with Uncle Paco?" asked María.

Manolo nodded. "Two men beat him up. He's hurt pretty bad."

"Then don't just stand there, *mi hijo,*" Concepción cried. "Bring him into the house."

"Uncle Paco, Uncle Paco," María wailed as José ran with his brother out to the cart.

"Poor old soul," Concepción murmured, looking down at the inert body being carried into the house. "Is he unconscious?"

"No," Manolo told her. "Asleep. My Angela fed him a big supper."

"Then why bring him way up here?" José asked.

"Because that's why he came stumbling to our house," Manolo answered. "He said Benito had to know it wasn't Paco's fault two men made off with *La Mariposa.*"

# chapter 15 ❧❧❧

Concepción woke up shortly before dawn, filled with the strong resolve that often follows a night spent tossing and turning. Things had gone far enough. In one day a group of half-crazed women had invaded her house, two savages had almost murdered her husband, and an outlaw had nailed a threat to her door. If that didn't justify a citizen's complaining to the mayor . . . Not that Pablo Estrada could do anything about the women or the hoodlums, but surely after all these years he could round up that band of smugglers. This very morning she would go down to the village and tell him so.

Her decision made, Concepción slipped out of bed, and in the gray light that filtered through the chinks in the shutters, padded to the wardrobe. Only the black dress seemed appropriate for a visit to the city hall, yet on touching the heavy cotton, her hand swerved rebelliously to the green satin.

A few minutes later, fully dressed, she crossed the main room, pausing en route to glance at the dark bulk that was the sleeping Manolo. *Pobrecito,* with only that thin blanket between him and the cold stone floor. Shivering in sympathy, she tiptoed to the kitchen, stepped across the sleeping José (whose bedroom had been given to Paco), opened the back door, and went out into the chill morning mist. How peaceful everything looked. As though spies and smugglers had disappeared with the darkness. But they hadn't, she reminded herself, and darted to the outhouse. And later, just as fast, back to the shelter of the cottage.

Inside the kitchen, she stopped at the pitcher for a token washing of her hands and face, then, with scarcely a glance in the mirror, wrapped her hair into a neat bun at the nape of her neck. Her ablutions complete, she picked up a pole and thumped on the ceiling to tell María del Carmen it was time to light the fire and prepare the morning chocolate. When the floorboards above her head creaked, she put the pole back in the corner and hurried to a moaning Paco Camino to assure him his friends were at hand and he could remain in bed as long as he wanted. At last, chores completed, she returned to the main room and touched Manolo lightly on the shoulder.

Instantly her son was awake, the result of countless similar awakenings on the open water. Yet though Manolo's body responded right away, his mind couldn't seem to grasp what she was saying. Pay a call on the mayor? Her? His mother?

"And what's so strange about that?" she asked, keeping her voice low so as not to waken Benito. "Am I not a citizen of this village? Has not my husband been beaten? A threatening letter nailed to my door?"

"*Sí, mamá,* but—"

"If your father were well, he would do this thing."

"He would?" Manolo left off scratching an armpit to gaze at her in wonder.

Concepción pursed her lips and considered the challenge. "Yes," she decided, "he would. Only later. When there was but one step between him and disaster."

That was the difference between her and her menfolk.

They delayed and talked things over; she forged ahead and got things done.

Later, over steaming mugs of chocolate, came the more difficult task of convincing José.

Demand the mayor take action against the smugglers, he asked. She must be crazy. Didn't the mayor, like all men in power, drink fine brandy and smoke imported cigars? Besides, what was she going to say if he accused her of attacking Father Juan?

"Father Juan had no right to bring those women into my bedroom."

"Or to tell the mayor the Bazáns are harboring stolen property?"

"Benito didn't steal those statues, and you know it."

"Yes, but does the mayor?"

Concepción squared her shoulders. "If the mayor's going to arrest me, it might as well be this morning."

"Why?" gasped José.

"Why not?" she snapped. Not being able to think of an answer. Sensing her plan was foolish, but determined to proceed with it, anyway.

Manolo looked up from cutting himself a chunk of bread. "I suppose you know, other than what Angela told me she heard at the fountain, I haven't the slightest idea what you two are talking about."

"That's all right, *mi hijo,*" Concepción said with an anxious glance at a yawning María del Carmen. "I'll tell you on the way to the village."

"Then you're going," said José.

"I have to," she declared. "It's my duty as a wife and as a . . . as a villager."

"A villager!" cried José. "*Mamá,* what's got into you?"

"I don't know," she said, pushing back her chair, "but I'm going, and that's all there is to it."

The last of the boats had already been beached when Concepción and Manolo arrived at *El Gran Gaitero*. From there, after thanking Eliseo for the loan of his cart, assuring him Paco was on the mend, declining for the moment an offer of coffee and a *churro,* Manolo headed for home and Concepción for the office of the mayor.

Halfway across the central plaza, she raised her eyes to the gray stone building directly in front of her. There was her destination: three arched windows behind a balcony draped with the blue and green flags of the *Romería*. Heart pounding, she passed beneath the pillared arcade, and after a brief pause to smooth her dress and arrange her shawl, mounted the stairs and opened the door marked ALCALDE.

The waiting room was empty and smelled of old upholstery and stale cigar smoke. Not sure whether she should sit down in one of the sagging armchairs or cross to the battered desk that guarded the entrance to the inner office, Concepción hesitated just inside the door. Except for the ticking of a clock, the room was silent. How long should she wait, she wondered, and glanced first at the time, then at a poster for the *Romería*. Music, dancing, gaiety, it said. Plus an unforgettable address by a member of the Cortés, the highly esteemed Octavio Mora.

"Is there something you want?" a voice called from across the room.

Concepción wheeled. Behind the battered desk stood a young man in a shiny black suit, staring at her disdainfully.

"Yes," she said. "I want to talk with Pablo Estrada, the mayor."

"About what?" The tone was insolent, as was the tilt of the young man's head.

Unsure what to say next, Concepción moved closer. Why, this young man was even younger than Manolo. What was she afraid of?

"Something personal," she said, drawing her shawl closer around her shoulders.

The clerk glanced at her wrinkled skirt and dusty espadrilles. "The name?"

"Concepción Peralta Soto de Bazán López."

With an expression that suggested such a name was hardly worth remembering, the clerk told her to wait, knocked on the mayor's door, and at a muffled command, went inside.

There was still time to run, Concepción thought, but before she could move, the youth was back, beckoning her to enter.

On trembling legs she started forward. The room was large, the furniture grand, the man behind the desk unexpectedly smiling.

"Ah, Señora Bazán," he said, gesturing to the chair across from him. "I was hoping one of you would come to see me, but frankly I thought it would be Benito."

"Benito's in bed," she said, stunned by the warm reception.

"Yes, I heard about what happened. Terrible, terrible. Any idea who those men were?"

"No, señor."

"The times we live in . . ." The mayor shook his well-groomed head. "Your husband's all right, I trust."

"Yes, Don Pablo. Just resting."

"Fine, fine." The mayor rubbed his hands together. "Well then, shall we get on with it?"

"I beg your pardon, señor?"

"Decide what's best for you and Benito to do."

"Then you know why I'm here," she gasped.

"Of course. To explain about the statues."

"Benito didn't steal them," she said, folding her hands tightly in her lap. "He just happened to look where nobody else had. And now El Chavo says they're his. But they aren't. And he has no right to kill him."

"Kill who?" asked the mayor, obviously confused.

"Benito. El Chavo's going to kill Benito. And it isn't right, señor. It isn't right."

The mayor leaned back and templed his fingers. "What do you expect me to do about this, Señora Bazán?"

"Catch him," she said. "Put him in prison."

"That's easier said than done, my good woman."

Concepción glanced at the mayor's watch, the box of cigars beside him on the desk, the wine and liquor on the cabinet behind him.

"It's not right," she repeated stubbornly. "Year after year, and all of us afraid. But nobody does anything."

"What are you saying, señora? That your mayor isn't doing his job?"

"Oh, no, señor."

"That's what it sounds like."

"Oh, no. I didn't mean . . . I just wanted—"

"What, señora? To tell me how to govern Amor Milagroso?" Face red, the mayor glared at her. "All right. You want me to do something. I'll do something. I'll put Benito and those statues in protective custody."

"Oh, no, señor. Please."

"Why not? That would keep him from being ambushed by smugglers. In fact, maybe I ought to put the whole village in protective custody, since according to you, every man, woman, and child is living in fear."

Concepción felt as though iron bands were being tightened across her chest. "Please, Don Pablo. Forgive me. It's just that the letter, and Benito moaning, and then those women . . . I didn't know what to do."

"Go home," sighed the mayor, seemingly drained of both color and energy. "And in the future, don't meddle in things that don't concern you."

Benito's life no concern to her?

"And my husband?" she asked, barely above a whisper.

"Tell him to stay home, too. I may want to speak with him."

Concepción froze. The mayor meant what he'd said. He was going to lock up Benito. Ay, what had she done? She had to get out of there. Warn him.

"Señora Bazán, are you all right?"

"Yes, Don Pablo. Fine, fine."

"Your face is the color of your dress."

"It's nothing. Please . . ."

Rising from her chair, she begged to be excused, and hurried to the door. Wondering as she turned the knob whether Benito, even if he escaped, could ever find it in his heart to forgive her.

"You can come out now, Father," said Pablo Estrada, and opened the door to the small alcove that served as his library. Father Juan was sitting near the window reading a thin, leather-bound book, the sun pouring on his head like a benediction.

What an inspiring picture, the mayor thought, then noticed the blush on the old priest's cheeks and wondered if he'd stumbled on the mayor's secret collection of erotica.

"She's gone, Father," the mayor said crisply. "You can—"

"Yes, yes, I heard you."

Father Juan snapped the book shut and pushed his body out of the armchair. "You have a fine collection of manuscripts here, my son."

"Since the death of my wife, books are my sole remaining passion," the mayor said dryly.

"So I see," the priest murmured, and waddling to the bookshelf, deftly replaced whatever it was he'd been reading. "I was particularly taken with a small volume describing the founding of our little village," he said, passing through the doorway. "You know, I'd quite forgotten that the exact site of the . . . ah . . . rejuvenation of Don Luis has never been officially determined."

"Is that so?" Pablo Estrada asked vaguely. Then, motioning to the chair vacated by Concepción, sat down at his desk and pulled nervously at his lower lip. So many things to worry about these days. Smugglers. Revolutionaries. Erotic treasures appearing out of nowhere . . .

"You seem troubled, my son. Do you want to talk about it?"

"Not particularly."

Thinking, even if he did put Benito in custody, he couldn't keep him there forever. Not with reform in the air . . .

"Let's go back to what you were telling me about those statues," he suggested.

"I think I'd finished, Pablo. Except to mention they're remarkable examples of Celtic craftsmanship."

"But where did he get them?"

The priest shook his head. "I haven't the slightest idea. But I can tell you this. If they're as old as I think, they might well be a national treasure. Which means the only place they rightfully belong is in a museum."

"One of yours, perhaps?"

"Perhaps . . ."

Not if I get there first, thought Pablo Estrada, and decided to round up some men and visit the Bazáns that very night.

# chapter 16

He felt a hundred years old, maybe a hundred and ten, but he had to make it to El Chavo's cave or die trying. What else could he do? Lie in bed and listen to Paco Camino snivel about his broken glasses, about being too sick to board the train for Milan? Complain. Complain. That was all Paco ever did. And all the while his pockets were stuffed with pesetas because Ramón and Pepe hadn't stolen the boat, they'd paid for it. And the train for Milan didn't even leave until tomorrow night. Whereas Benito . . . ay, there was someone with problems! A battered body. Cutthroats waiting to kill him. A wife who . . . no, he didn't even want to think about it. Imagine, going off to see the mayor without so much as a word. By heaven, a man had his pride.

Panting heavily, he crested the hill, and favoring his bad knee, limped off on a zigzag course through the oak trees. Soon, if memory served him, he'd see the scattered ruins that marked the entrance to the vaulted chamber. Then, God willing, someone would open the trapdoor, come out of the cave, and take him to see El Chavo.

Five years had passed since the morning after the storm, when they had spoken to one another on a deserted beach. El Chavo must be—what? Sixty? Sixty-five? Yet in Benito's mind he was still the hot-blooded young man who, on learning his wife had been killed while visiting her parents in Guernica, quit his job at the bank and walked into the hills to join the local band of outlaws. Benito always thought that because El Chavo had a crippled right hand, he'd felt this was the only way he could strike back: to abandon both sides and operate—strictly for profit—somewhere in the middle.

Wiping his brow, Benito wondered what his own life would have been like if that day on the beach he'd joined the outlaws as El Chavo had suggested. Would he now be living in a fine house, drinking liquor and smoking cigars? Or would he be shivering in some hut, waiting to sail into the fog and receive another shipment? Hard work, smuggling. Like fishing. Only besides the cold and the storms, a man also had to worry about bullets. And there was always the chance of ending his days in some dark, airless prison.

He shivered, and glimpsing the ruins up ahead, sank down beneath an enormous oak tree. Except for the buzzing of bees, the grove was silent. Too silent. What should he do, he wondered. Sit patiently and wait? Call out? Or approach the trapdoor, and if no one came out, go down in the cave on his own? It would be frightening, creeping down those stairs, not knowing who or what waited at the bottom. But it was also frightening to sit out here among the trees, a perfect target for—

"All right. Hands above your head!" called a voice, harsh and commanding.

Benito shuddered. Did as he was told.

"What do you want?" the voice demanded.

"Tell El Chavo I've come about his letter."

"Bring anything with you?"

Benito licked his lips. "I answer questions only of your leader."

"I'll remember that, Benito Bazán," snarled the voice. "All right. On your feet."

Benito got up, in the process peering cautiously over his shoulder. Beside an oak, above the barrel of a rifle, a man in black was glaring at him.

"That way," the man growled, pointing with his gun to a hill beyond the grove.

"But that's not the way to—"

"Start walking!"

"But where—"

"I don't answer questions, either, *amigo*. Move!"

So saying, the man walked forward. A burly giant with a jagged scar on his left cheek and a golden earring in his left ear.

"El Bruto," Benito gasped, and limped as fast as he could into the underbrush. Branches clawed at his overalls; leaves and twigs crunched under his boots. Where was the beast taking him, he wondered, and once they got there . . .

Without warning, at the base of a rocky hill, El Bruto pushed past and started climbing. Panting and sweating, Benito followed as best he could, slipping on stones, clinging frantically to boulders and bushes. At last he crawled to the summit and peered down the opposite slope. On a grassy ledge some fifty meters below, El Bruto waited with his rifle.

"Over there!" he barked, pointing to eight thatch-roofed huts that looked out over a seemingly endless expanse of rolling hills and wooded valleys.

Fear skittered down Benito's backbone. Except for El Bruto, there wasn't a sign of a human being anywhere.

"NOW!" El Bruto yelled, and Benito started down,

terrified at the prospect of being alone with that beast in one of those isolated pagan huts.

Concepción knelt in the stuffy dimness, her heart beating more calmly, but her mind still far from serene. If only she hadn't believed it was her duty to think for the entire family, if only she'd revealed her plan to Benito, he'd have forbidden her to talk with the mayor, and that would have been that. Hers had been a sin of pride. A belief she was her husband's equal and could do as he did. Never again would she harbor such a sinful idea. And what, she wondered, had made her harbor it this time?

Folding her hands on the railing before the altar, Concepción raised her eyes to the statue of the Virgin, She of the blue velvet cloak who waited with open arms to embrace all who strayed from the fold and returned repentant. And Concepción had strayed from the fold. Sins of omission, sins of commission . . . how was she ever going to atone for all she had done? One thing. The moment she got home, she'd fling herself at Benito's feet and beg his forgiveness.

Lowering her eyes, she began mumbling a fervent Hail Mary, but while her lips mouthed the words, her mind asked: Are you really repentant? Really and truly repentant?

She stopped chanting. Raised her head. Useless to pray; her mind was in a thousand places at once. What she'd do was compose herself and go home.

Clutching her shawl, she got to her feet, crossed to a row of rickety chairs, and sat down. Behind her, Tía Rosa's shovel grated and clanged on the uneven stone floor as the old woman scraped away yesterday's candle wax. Strange they let Tía Rosa work in the church when everyone knew she was a witch. But who was Concepción to judge? Nobody kept a sinner like her from coming in, either.

The scraping stopped, and Tía Rosa, minus her shovel, made a sudden beeline for the altar. There, without hesitation, she flung a black-stockinged leg over the rail, hunched the rest of her body after, then dropped to her knees and with clawlike hands reached up to stroke the blue velvet cloak.

Concepción flinched. Never had she liked exaggerated displays of religious devotion—flagellants lashing themselves with whips, women shrieking when the crucified wooden Christ passed them in a procession. Yet as she watched Tía Rosa kissing the statue's feet, it struck Concepción she planned to engage in a similar display when she got home. No, she decided. I'm not like that. I'll never be able to do it.

Feeling strangely calm, she got to her feet, left the row of chairs, and after genuflecting to the Virgin and the spellbound (or sleeping) figure at Her feet, turned and hurried to the door. What she had to do was tell Benito what the mayor had said, then, together with José, work out a plan of action. Which must include a phone call to Don Miguel to prevent him from doing anything foolish, should Benito run away.

She stepped out into the street, blinking in the sudden sunlight. Why, it was barely noon, she saw on the clock above the *farmacia*. Barely noon and there she was, only minutes from *El Gran Gaitero*. So to save José the trip later this afternoon, why not take five minutes and—much as she hated to do it—call Don Miguel herself?

Above his head, dry thatch. Beneath his boots, rough stones. Behind him, the muzzle of a rifle; in front, a raised trapdoor and a flight of stairs, leading downward.

"All right, *amigo*, move!" El Bruto barked, and Benito hobbled down the steps, through a doorway, and into an enormous room, where he stopped short, gaping at sofas, lamps, Oriental rugs, plus wall-to-ceiling windows looking out over hills and valleys.

"Ah, Benito, come in," called a familiar voice, and Benito wheeled to see a bald-headed man in a black suit, white shirt, and tie, sitting behind a desk smoking a cigar.

"Sit down, my friend, sit down," the smuggler said, and Benito limped across the room to an armchair worthy of Queen Isabella.

"I was just enjoying the first cigar of the afternoon," El Chavo announced, as with his one good hand he tapped his ash into a silver ashtray. "I'm getting old, Benito. My doctor says I have to watch how much I smoke. So that's what I do. I watch and I count." He threw back his head and laughed. "Sometimes I even write the number down. It makes him furious."

Benito stared at El Chavo's bare skull, clipped eyebrows, trim mustache, wondering what had become of the shaggy-haired bandit who used to ride through the night with a dagger strapped to his calf and a pistol tucked in his cummerbund.

"What about you?" the smuggler asked. "Are you, too, at the mercy of your doctor?"

Benito shook his head.

"Wonderful!" Setting aside his cigar, El Chavo raised the lid of a large wooden box. "These are the finest on the market. Take one and savor that— Wait a minute. What happened to your forehead?"

"Nothing, nothing. A brief encounter with . . . with Engracia."

"Still capable of the old amusements, eh?"

"*Hombre,* Engracia is my cow."

"Well, *chacun à son goût,* as the French say."

As the French say? What was this?

El Chavo held out the wooden box. "You don't want one?"

"*Gracias.* Not at the moment." At the moment, if he let go of his chair, he'd collapse on the carpet in a heap.

"Well, then, other than having been kicked by a cow, how are you?"

"Fine, fine."

"Farm work still agree with you?"

"As much as ever."

"You still see our old friend Tomás?"

"Tomás and his brother are working up in Germany."

"And Jorge?"

"A hotel clerk up in England."

"So many of the old group gone," El Chavo sighed. "Life is hard, Benito."

"Not for you, it seems."

"I have my burdens."

"We all do, Vicente."

"Vicente . . ." The smuggler leaned back and exhaled a cloud of cigar smoke. "Nobody's called me that since before the war. That blasted war." He glared at the hand lying useless on the desk. "With Cervantes it was at least his left," he said bitterly. "They called him the 'Maimed One,' did you know that?"

Benito grunted. "I must have forgotten."

"Me they call a thief and a murderer. Ha! I'm not a murderer, I'm a one-armed bandit." He laughed. "Do you know what those words mean in English, Benito? A machine people put money in, hoping to gain a profit. What they forget is, the machine's inner workings are beyond their control."

Benito nodded, wondering when he should bring up the subject of the letter.

"I learn such things in books," El Chavo continued. "Look around. I have quite a library, *verdad?*"

Benito turned his throbbing head. The smuggler was right; two entire walls were lined with bookcases.

"I started by importing a few choice items from France for some of my special customers," El Chavo explained. "Then before I knew it, I was importing things for myself. It's amazing how forbidden books, especially the ones with pictures, inspire a man to read faster and better."

Benito cocked an ear to an archway across the room. Was he more feverish than he thought, or was someone beyond that arch playing a piano?

"You used to be a good reader, Benito. Remember when that letter came for your father? You were the only one in the family who could read it."

"Sometimes I think it would have been better if I couldn't," Benito muttered, remembering his father striding from the house to disappear forever into the fog and darkness.

"Who's to say," El Chavo murmured. "That was forty years ago. Now here we are. Me commanding an army of outlaws. You accused by that army of invading its territory and making off with one of its treasures."

Here we go, thought Benito, and taking a firm hold on the arms of his chair, said, "You didn't know that treasure existed until people in the village started talking."

"A possession is a possession, Benito. Something another man has no right to remove. Especially when he's trespassing."

"Bah. You don't own that cave any more than I do."

El Chavo crushed out his cigar. "Don't try my patience,

Benito. Are you going to give back those statues or aren't you?"

Benito licked his feverish lips. "Those figures belong to me," he said. "I found them and I intend to—"

"Those figures are mine!" El Chavo roared. "Now where are they?"

"Where you and your men will never find them," Benito lied.

"I see. And I suppose if something happens to you, your friends have certain instructions."

"Naturally." Wishing that were true.

"Believe me, Benito, when El Bruto has orders to find something, there isn't a man on this earth who can refuse to tell him where it's hidden."

Much less a woman, Benito thought, and the image of El Bruto storming into the house, attacking Concepción, was so unbearable, tears spilled from his already watery eyes.

"*Oye, amigo,*" he croaked, "maybe there's a way we could—"

"Turn that accursed thing off!" El Chavo thundered, as beyond the arch the tinkling piano changed to screeching voices and twanging guitars. "Young people," he muttered. "I wonder if they know what that music of theirs does to us."

"Hard to say . . . but to get on with my proposition. Listen, Vicente, do you have any idea what those statues could be worth?"

El Chavo smiled. "Why do you think I'm so determined to get them back?"

"Only a rich foreigner could afford to buy a treasure like that," Benito declared, "and that's exactly what I've found: a rich foreigner."

"You, Benito?"

"Don't laugh, *amigo*. I, too, am a man of business."

"All right, so you've got a buyer. What's that to me?"

"Spare my life and I'll give you half of what he pays me."

"Settle for half when the statues are mine?"

"Kill me and you won't receive a centavo."

"We'll see."

Benito swallowed dryly. "My buyer arrives the tenth of July. Do you want to be there, or don't you?"

"You haven't been listening, my friend. I said it's all or nothing."

"I can't give you all," Benito wailed. "Half already goes to Don Miguel."

"Don Miguel! You made an arrangement with Don Miguel?"

"I had to. Otherwise he would have taken me and my statues to the police."

"No, my friend. Not Don Miguel. He has too many debts to let a source of income escape him like that."

El Chavo reached in the wooden box for the second cigar of the afternoon. "Bah, what a man of business. With what your partner gives you, you'll be lucky to buy Concepción a new dress and yourself a bottle or two of wine."

All at once Benito felt sick to his stomach. No matter what he did, he was going to get cheated. As always. It wasn't fair. A man worked for years and . . . but no, he hadn't worked for those statues, he'd stumbled on them by accident. No, that wasn't right, either. He'd been led to that cave by the fox . . . and then there was that ray of sunshine . . .

"Benito! What's wrong with you?"

He shivered. Shook his head. The smuggler was either going to kill him or take away his treasure. Either way, Benito was going to lose. As he'd lost the *A Mi Gusto* and *La Mariposa* and . . . and . . .

"*Hombre,* what is it? You look as though you're dying."

Benito tried to focus his eyes, but no matter what he did, he kept seeing El Chavo through a shimmering green haze. Maybe because both of them were underwater. Yes, that was it. The smuggler was wrong. Benito wasn't dying, he was already dead.

# chapter 17

A knock sounded on the door, and José stalked across the room to answer it. Outside, three men stood on the doorstep in the gathering darkness.

"*Buenas noches.* Is Benito here?" asked a tall, mournful man who José vaguely remembered sold vegetables in the central market.

José shook his head. "What's going on? Why are so many men asking to see my father?"

"There are only three of us," snapped Tío Arturo, the white-haired uncle of Eliseo Rabal.

"I can see that," José said testily, "but look over there." He pointed to the barn, where some twenty-five men stood clustered around their burros, laughing and talking.

"Quite a crowd," murmured Ignacio León, husband to the sharp-tongued Teresa. "And there are even more coming up the road behind us."

"But what is it you all want?" José demanded. "Nobody will tell me. Have you come to mourn him, is that it? Has

somebody found my father's body and is afraid to tell me?"
The tall man frowned. "Benito's body?"

"We didn't even know he was dead," said Tío Arturo.
"We came to see those indecent statues."

"Our wives are driving us crazy," the tall man said,
lowering his voice in deference to María del Carmen, who was
sitting at the table, darning José's socks. "Ever since yesterday afternoon we can't get them out of the bedroom."

"Not that we're complaining," Ignacio added. "Thirty-
five years and this is the first time Teresa has ever asked for
it."

"So that's why we're here," the tall man whispered. "We
thought if we could see those golden lovers for ourselves,
well, we might feel more inspired."

"Inspired, bah," grumbled Tío Arturo. "We just hope we
can keep up the pace."

"What's all the talking?" Concepción called from the
bedroom. "Is he back? Is he all right?"

"No, mamá," José shouted over his shoulder. "It's just
another group from the village. Stay there and rest."

Angrily, he turned back to the waiting threesome. "The
people in this house are sick with worry, and you come here
asking about statues. Have you no shame, no sense of—"

"What's going on? Who are all these people?" croaked
Paco Camino as, arms outstretched, he came stumbling
across the room like a befuddled sleepwalker.

"Nobody, old man," called José. "Go back to bed."

"What's Paco Camino doing here in his underwear?" asked
Ignacio León.

"Yes, why can Paco see the statues and not us?" whined Tío
Arturo.

"Nobody's seeing the statues," José cried, starting to close
the door, "so you can tell your friends in the—"

"*Oye,* Paco," yelled Tío Arturo, jamming his foot between the door and the frame. "Have you seen them? What did they do for you?"

"Nothing!" José shouted. Kicked away the foot and slammed the door.

"What was that about statues?" Paco asked as he followed José to the table.

"Nothing, nothing," the young man murmured.

"Don't lie to me, José. I heard them. And you, too."

"Please, *viejo,* go back to bed."

"Not until you tell me what they were talking about."

"Could it be those golden figures in your parents' bedroom?" María del Carmen asked shyly.

"Aha. So you have seen them," said José.

María blushed and lowered her eyes. "I know it was wrong, but one day when your mother and father went out to the fields . . ."

"I know. You tiptoed into the room and pulled away the red velvet cloth."

"How did you know?" she gasped.

"It's a logical thing to do."

"It seems to me," Paco muttered, "that if a man owns some golden figures, the least he can do is show them to his oldest and most intimate friend."

"That's something you'll have to discuss with my father," said José. "Assuming the poor man is still alive."

"Are you that worried, José?"

"Five hours I've searched, and not a trace of him."

Another knock sounded on the door, and Paco's eyes blazed with excitement.

"That's him this time, José. I can feel it."

"Maybe so, but if it's Father, why would he knock?" the young man asked as he hurried to the door, prepared to give a verbal lashing to the first man who even mentioned the word statues. Instead, he found himself gaping at an empty step, a dark yard, and a shadowy figure sprinting across the cabbage patch.

"Wait! Stop!" José yelled, and leaping from the step, gave chase across the yard, wishing he had a gun, a club, a light—anything. Voices called to him from the barn, while ahead the running figure was joined by somebody else and together they sped toward the distant hillside. José quickened his pace, aware of cabbages squashing beneath his feet, the surrounding landscape growing darker and darker. Suddenly he spied a shadowy mass huddled against the wall to the vineyard, swerved from his course, and darted toward it.

"*Papá,*" he cried. Then, sinking to his knees, pulled the cloth from his father's mouth and began untying the ropes that bound his arms.

"Benito, I'm not exaggerating," Concepción insisted. "You can't just sit there. Pablo Estrado is going to put you and those statues in—"

"According to José, those men have been waiting since sundown."

"I'm not worried about those men, I'm worried about you."

"So worried you stole from my bed to go visit your friend the mayor."

"And you stole off to— Benito, you could have been killed up there and none of us would have known the difference."

"Calm yourself, woman," Benito muttered, breaking off another hunk of bread. "Am I not a man? I know how to take care of myself."

"Ha! Wait until the police come and—"

"Well, well, here are my friends from the village. Come in, dear friends, come in."

"Benito, are you all right?" asked Ignacio León, crossing from the door to the table.

"José said you were dead," Tío Arturo reported.

"Obviously José was wrong," Benito said. "As you can see, I'm fine. Perfectly fine."

Though in truth his trip up the hill and his encounter with El Chavo had left him a bit shaky. Nothing serious, of course. He'd get over it, thanks to those seven hours in one of the smuggler's fancy bedrooms. Strange El Chavo should have done that. Put Benito to bed, let him sleep away his shock and his fever. And what a fever! At one time Benito even imagined the smuggler leaning over the bed, telling him things were going to work out fine. Which they certainly weren't. Not for Benito, at least. He knew the smuggler had sent him home with those men in hopes they could force him to hand over the treasure. Never dreaming that so many of Benito's friends would be waiting outside the house.

"That's right, my friends, move in close," he said, rising to his feet and pushing aside his chair as the newest arrivals began crowding against those in the front row.

"How much longer will we have to wait?" someone called from the doorway.

"No time at all," Benito called back. "José, bring out the golden statues."

"*Papá*, are you sure it's wise to—"

"The women saw them, didn't they? And the priest and the mayor and God knows—"

"The mayor hasn't seen them," Concepción broke in.

"Was that because you left in such a hurry you forgot to take them with you?"

Concepción sucked in her breath and without another word stalked to the opposite side of the table, the men moving aside so she could get a place in the front row.

"Some people never show anybody anything," Paco muttered, drawing a blanket closer around his shoulders. "Not even their oldest and closest friends."

"And why should they," Benito snapped, "when their oldest and closest friends sell their prized possessions to somebody else?"

José touched his father's shoulder. "Please, *papá*. The old one has had a bad day. Every time he fell asleep he was awakened by a nightmare."

"Proof it's time he rose from his bed and headed for the train station."

"If Paco feels weak, Paco will remain here," Concepción said firmly.

"Within the hour my wife will be dishing up broiled sausages and a potato omelet," Tío Arturo announced. "So tell me, Benito, are you going to show us this indecent thing or aren't you?"

"I am," Benito replied. "José, do as I told you."

"*Sí, papá.*"

Muttering under his breath the young man left the room, returning a few seconds later with a velvet-draped bundle which he resolutely set down in front of his father.

"Now, then, *amigos*," Benito began, surveying the ring of eager faces, "many of you have been wondering why lights burn all night in the bedroom of the Bazáns."

"Benito, please," Concepción protested.

"She's right," someone called, "pull off that cloth and be done with it."

"Just what I was about to do," Benito said. And did so.

There was an awed silence, followed by a low rumble as the men in the back began elbowing aside those in the front.

"No need to push," Benito said. "Here. Pass them around."

"Ay, Benito," croaked the farmer next to him, "what are these things made of? My fingers burn as though I'd placed them in a fire."

"That's because they're . . . how old, José?"

"Over twenty-five hundred years," José replied, "which is why you should be careful how you—"

"Nonsense! Enjoy them!" Benito commanded. "After tonight we may never see them again."

"Why is that?" asked Ignacio León, passing the twosome to the man next to him.

"Pablo Estrada's going to lock them up," Concepción said dryly.

"Oh, no, he's not," Benito declared. "So don't worry, my friends, just—"

"Ay, Pedro! You broke it!" somebody shouted. "Look. The man and the woman are no longer together."

"That's all right," Benito told him, "I was going to show you that later."

"Mother of God," breathed a scrawny old fisherman, "look at that little fellow's equipment."

"And look at those ears," the man next to him exclaimed. "By heaven, he's got stick-out ears just like Benito."

"The size of the ears may be the same," another man added, "but not the size of something else."

"How do you know?" croaked the fisherman.

"It's time for us to leave," Concepción announced, and grabbing María del Carmen by the arm, marched her across the room and up the stairs to the loft. Meanwhile the figures—now joined, now separated—continued their tour of the table until, all in one piece, they reached the trembling hands of Paco Camino.

"Remind you of the old days, *viejo?*" Tío Arturo asked with a toothless leer.

"*Hombre,* for the love of heaven," Paco moaned, lifting the couple to within an inch of his eyes, "don't torture a man who can barely see them."

"Pull them apart," somebody hollered.

Paco did, and cackling obscenely, looked first at the strutting male in his left hand, then at the backbending female in his right.

"Wait a minute," Benito yelled over the guffaws and catcalls. "Quiet! I thought I heard something."

"A car," somebody cried.

"Quick! Paco. Snap them together," Benito shouted.

"I told you," Concepción called as she came running down the stairs. "It's the police. I know it."

"Here, José," cried Benito. "Hide them!"

José grabbed the statues and passed them to his mother, who in turn ran to the kitchen and plunged them in a pot of dried beans.

Knuckles rapped on the door.

"Come back," Benito called as the men surged toward the kitchen. "You've done nothing wrong."

"Since when does that make any difference?" a farmer called over his shoulder.

"Benito Bazán!" a voice shouted from outside the front door. "Open to us at once!"

"Ay, there's someone at the back door, too," a man wailed from the kitchen.

"There, you see, there's no escape," Benito sighed. And

feeling very old and very tired, told his son to open the door and let whoever was out there come in.

Flanked by two men in wrinkled brown uniforms, Pablo Estrada, a camel's hair coat draped casually across his shoulders, sauntered into the room, his eyes sweeping the men who had lined up against the walls as if expecting to be shot.

"I seem to be interrupting some sort of meeting," he said with a twisted smile.

"No, no," Benito assured him, "my friends just heard I was unwell and came out to the farm to see me."

"Ah, yes, your wife told me you were ill. You're better now, though, I trust."

"Yes, Don Pablo, much better. In fact, my friends were just leaving."

"I hope I haven't chased them away," the mayor said. Then, smile gone, he nodded to his men, who promptly drew their guns and stationed themselves at either side of the door.

"Is something wrong, Don Pablo?" Benito asked, pretending a calm he in no way felt.

"Probably not," the mayor replied, "but there are things one has to investigate." He smiled briefly, then straightened his shoulders and cleared his throat. "Father Juan tells me you have a statue here that may well be a national treasure. I'd like to see it."

"Are you an expert, señor?"

"I beg your pardon?"

"An expert. That's what it takes to inspect a work of art. Unless, of course, one is talking about folk art. Folk art can be judged by—"

"Benito, I'm warning you."

"Yes, señor?"

"Give me that golden statue."

"And if I refuse?"

"I'm not asking you, I'm telling you."

José touched his father's arm. "Shouldn't he have some papers, *papá?*"

"I don't know, *mi hijo*, should he?"

"*Sí,* Benito, *sí,*" called a few voices from the walls.

"At least ask him to write these things down," someone suggested.

"And get a receipt," suggested someone else.

"Benito doesn't need a receipt," Ignacio León declared. "Look around. He's got more than two dozen witnesses."

"Witnesses!" snorted Tío Arturo. "What good are they? Remember after the war?"

"Times have changed," said a youth with tousled black hair. "Witnesses no longer are afraid to testify."

"Is that so?" Pablo Estrada asked softly.

"Today there are ways to protest," the youth went on. "Ways that can be very effective if someone of importance is known to be watching. Octavio Mora, for example."

"Bah," said the old fisherman. "Why should a man like Mora care what happens to Benito and his statues?"

"He'd have to care if the whole time he was in Amor Milagroso, bombs kept exploding outside his window."

"You realize, young man," the mayor said, "I could arrest you right now for provoking a revolution. For the time being, however, I'm going to content myself with taking note of your name."

"Pedro Pérez," the young man said proudly.

"I'll remember that. And now my patience is running out. Benito, bring me that statue."

"Benito! No!" cried Concepción. "Don Miguel won't allow it. I know. I talked with him on the telephone."

"My God, what else did you do today?" Benito groaned.

"Señora Bazán, what are you saying?" the mayor asked. "That if Benito gives me the statue, Don Miguel will . . . what?"

"I don't know, señor. He just said that if the mayor proved to be a problem—those were his very words, Don Pablo—if the mayor proved to be a problem, Don Miguel and his father would know what to do about it."

"I see," said Pablo Estrada. "Then it seems it's time Miguel and I had a little talk." He signaled to his men, who put away their guns and opened the door. "Don't think you two have won," the mayor called from the threshold. "Your friends aren't going to be concerned about Benito's health forever."

"I'm not sure, Don Pablo," Benito said with a smile. "Tomorrow morning, for example, the fishermen who now are out on their boats will doubtless be coming to see me. Followed by the women who weren't here yesterday. And then the men who weren't here today. And then, *quién sabe?* But it wouldn't surprise me if, day or night, one could visit this farm and never find Benito and his statues alone."

# chapter 18 🌺🌺

José rolled onto his back and willed his body to relax. Useless. The blanket still resembled a tent with one sturdy tent pole.

He sighed and looked at the glowing numbers on his watch. Four in the morning. What was he going to do? Splash himself with water? Go out for a walk?

Flipping back the covers, he stood naked beside the cot, peering into the darkness. That bundle over by the cupboard was his clothes; that shadow outside the window, one of the men who had elected to remain on guard. If José went out, the man would be startled, cry out, wake the rest of the family. Besides, it would be damp out there, and cold.

He shivered, yanked the blanket off his bed, and wrapped it around him like a cloak. Then he tiptoed across the kitchen, cocked an ear to the other room, and satisfied everyone was asleep, started up the stairs to the loft.

Benito opened his eyes. Strange, he thought he'd heard something. By heaven, he was restless tonight. Maybe he should get up and have a smoke.

Easing out of bed, he padded to the other room and sat down at the big round table. What a day this had been . . . and what a night. Life certainly wasn't what it used to be.

He felt on the table for his cigarettes, then found and struck a match. It was pleasant, this sitting alone in the darkness. He felt like a shepherd guarding his flock against wolves. No, not just against wolves. Against dogs, cats, foxes, rabbits—everything that moved. And the prize was far more than a sheep.

He yawned, scratched his belly, thinking tomorrow he'd have to get those golden figures out of the bedroom. Maybe Concepción would know where to hide them. She seemed to know everything else these days. Quite a woman, that Concepción. When he got back in bed, he'd have to see if she was feeling restless, too.

•

José stood beside the bed and stared down at the bundle under the blankets. In the dim moonlight, all he could see clearly was her face. Even that made his heart beat wildly.

"Come on, María," he whispered. "Girls in Madrid do it all the time."

"Catholic girls?" she gasped.

"My God, don't you feel any urge at all?"

"I—I don't know. What does an urge feel like?"

He frowned, searching for an easy—but above all, quick—explanation. "You feel tense. Nervous. Sometimes you even twitch."

"Ay, that was how I felt when I first saw the golden statues."

"Tense and twitchy?"

"*Sí*, José, *sí*."

"Where?"

"I told you. In your parents' bedroom."

He gritted his teeth. "No, I mean where on your body?"

"All over, but mostly, well, right around here."

He saw a thin white hand come out from under the covers and hover in the vicinity of his target.

"What did you do?" he asked, sitting gingerly on the bed.

"Nothing," she breathed.

"In truth, María?"

There was a moment's silence; then, so softly he could barely hear: "I—I put my hand there."

"And then?"

"It was strange. Like being pricked by a thousand tiny needles. Then I began to shiver."

"And then?" he whispered against her hair.

"Then I looked out the window and saw your father and mother returning from the fields."

112

"Oh, María," he moaned, stretching out beside her. "Wouldn't you like to know what comes after all those chills and twitches? Wouldn't you, María?"

"I—I don't know. I've never— While you've probably— And we haven't even talked about getting married."

"For God's sake, María."

"Maybe if we were at least *thinking* about it . . ."

"I think about it all the time," he lied.

"You do?"

"Yes, yes. Oh, yes, María, yes." Scarcely daring to breathe, he folded back the blanket and ran quivering fingers along the base of her throat.

"Oh, you're so beautiful, so beautiful," he whispered, then leaned over and kissed her on the lips. What did it matter if she'd never finished school, never traveled beyond Galicia. She was young, she was desirable—and most important—she was here.

Gathering courage, he scrambled to his feet and flipped the blanket completely off her. Was this what he wanted? To marry María and live forever on his grandfather's farm?

She moaned. Lifted up her arms.

Nothing is forever, José told himself. And holding his blanket by the corners, fluttered batlike down onto the bed.

Benito crushed out his cigarette. He felt tired now, ready for a few hours sleep.

Halfway to the bedroom, he cocked an ear to the ceiling. Creaking bedsprings. María del Carmen must be restless, too.

He smiled and continued on his way, thinking, strange José hadn't come out to see who was prowling around the main room. The boy must really be exhausted. Either that or . . . no, he wouldn't dare. But just to make sure . . .

"Oh, José, José . . . the chills, they're coming back."
"Here. Feel this. This will cure them."
"Ay, it's so big," she gasped. "However will we—"
"It's nothing, nothing." Amazed he'd ever argue for smallness. "Here, just move this leg over to—"
"*José! What in the name of God are you doing?*" Benito roared.
José went limp. Rolled off the girl; then, clutching his blanket, staggered to his feet.
"*Papá!*"
"Right! And what about the girl? By heaven, if you've—"
"No, no. She's fine, she's fine."
"Is that true, María del Carmen?" Benito demanded.
"Oh, Señor Bazán, Señor Bazán," she wailed, tears streaming down her cheeks.
"Mother of God," he breathed. "José, get down those stairs before I'm tempted to kill you."

Sitting on the bed, Concepción regarded the girl standing by the window, gazing listlessly out at the sunrise.
"What I'm trying to say, María my dear, is that since nothing really happened, you don't have to marry him. Not if you don't want to. Not if you don't love him."
The girl turned, her cheeks wet with tears. "But I do, I do."
"Ah, yes," Concepción said softly. "Then you must make sure José loves you in return. Otherwise what you build together will be false."
The girl ran to the bed, and sinking to her knees, grabbed

Concepción's hand. "I know that, señora. But José does love me. He does. I'm sure of it."

Concepción sighed, and with her free hand, patted the girl on the head. Might as well try to reason with the wind.

# PART III ❧❧

# chapter 19

On the tenth of July, dark clouds hung low over Galicia, occasionally spilling their contents on hills and valleys, inlets and beaches.

One such downpour awakened Benito shortly before dawn. He opened an eye. Was glad to find he was still in his bed, for he'd dreamed he was on the sea, fighting wind and waves as he waited for that inevitable screech of wood against rock. Foul nightmare. One would think the day he was to sell his treasure, his dreams would be more agreeable.

He yawned, scratched, rolled over onto his side.

"Uh, eh," Concepción mumbled. "Are they here?"

"Ay, *mujer,* do the sons of dukes and the buyers of statues emerge from their beds earlier than we do? We won't see them until ten, maybe eleven o'clock this morning."

"Uh," she grunted. "I thought I heard shouting."

He cocked an ear. "Pilgrims!" he cried, and swinging his

legs to the floor, thanked God this was the last day he'd have to sneak out before dawn and retrieve the lovers from the secret hiding place.

Shortly before noon a silver-gray Ferrari emerged from the driveway of the villa, turned east, and roared along the road that skirted the coast all the way to Pontevedra. Behind the wheel sat the trim-bearded Don Miguel, and beside him a clean-shaven blond who with the two women in the back seat had arrived the previous night from London.

"How long a trip is it?" one of the women—a buxom, middle-aged redhead—asked in English.

"Twenty minutes or so," answered Don Miguel, "but with all this rain . . ."

"Can we eat up there?" asked the blond man.

Don Miguel laughed. "You can if they invite you, but you're liable to get pork with turnip tops or maybe black bread and a steamed potato."

"I thought this coast was noted for its seafood," the blond man said, flicking the ash from his pungent black cigarette.

"My dear Erik," the driver replied, "if you wanted seafood, you should have told me. Our housekeeper always has an octopus or two in the freezer. And eels. As I remember, you Danes are wild about eels."

"I'd like to try some *merluza*," said the fourth member of the group, a woman about thirty with shoulder-length, chestnut-colored hair, green eyes, and a woebegone expression. "Or what else is special here?" she went on. "*Caldo gallego? Nécoras?*"

"Wow! Gabrielle!" cried the redhead. "Where'd you learn all that?"

"In a guidebook, Aunt Iris."

"Yes, but your pronunciation. *Nécoras,*" she repeated, hitting the accented *e* so hard she set her dangle earrings to quivering.

"Come on, Aunt Iris. You know I speak Spanish."

"And quite enchantingly," the driver put in. "In fact, I feel so enchanted that—rain or no rain—I've decided to drive farther up the coast and take you all to one of my favorite little restaurants. The seafood is excellent, the wines superb, and the *ambiente* . . . well, it's so *típico* you'll hardly be able to stand it."

"But what about the farmer?" asked Gabrielle. "Won't he be waiting?"

"Of course. But that's no problem, Señora Van der Linden. We'll get there eventually."

"I know, only . . ."

The driver laughed. "Rest assured, dear lady. For Miguel Granflaqueza and his friends, that farmer will be willing to wait forever."

It rained most of the day, but around three o'clock the clouds began to thin and a timid sun poked through the overcast. A good omen, thought Benito, as for the twentieth time since noon he stood on the doorstep looking for the car that must surely arrive within the next five minutes.

And when it did, he realized, gazing at the pilgrims milling around the wood-and-canvas booths, the families talking under the fruit trees, the old women sitting gossiping on bales of hay—when the car did come, all this was going to end. No more oxcarts, trucks, cars, and buses would come pulling into the yard every hour of the day and night; no more pilgrims would sleep in the barn, wash in the laundry shed, eat wherever they could find room. It was going to be hard leading a quiet, ordinary life again, but at least he wouldn't have to keep crawling out of bed before daybreak to smuggle the little figures into the house, then pretend to take them from the cast-iron box chained to the dentist's chair.

He sighed, and flipping his cigarette into a nearby puddle, raised his eyes to the distant hillside. Strange, in all these days not a sign of El Chavo. That must mean he'd taken Benito's proposition seriously, and the minute Don Miguel arrived, would come charging into the room, demanding his fair share of the profits. Well, better that than the statues themselves, Benito thought, and turned back to the driveway in time to see Paco Camino start flailing his arms and jumping up and down.

Now what was that all about, Benito wondered, and hurried through the crowd to find the old fisherman directing a bright red Seat into a space barely wide enough for a couple of motorcycles.

"Stop! Stop!" Benito yelled at the driver, then turned to the protesting Paco. "*Amigo,* I've told you a thousand times. Not so close together."

Paco frowned and studied the parking place. "That doesn't look close to me," he declared.

"Assuming the car got in there, how would the passengers get out?"

"Ah. That I never thought of."

"You never do. Doubtless because you, yourself, have never driven."

"And have you, Benito? Have you?"

"That's beside the point," Benito muttered, and bending to the window of the Seat, suggested the driver and his family might feel more at ease if they stationed their vehicle over by the grain shed. The driver agreed, and the Seat was bouncing across the yard when Paco grabbed his friend by the forearm.

"Look! There he comes!"

Benito wheeled. Chugging up the hill was an ancient orange bus with LAS PALOMILLAS printed above the windshield.

"Paco, my friend," he sighed, "it's clear the time has come for you to seek out another pair of glasses."

Paco pushed up the square lenses rimmed with tortoise-shell. "These are fine spectacles, Benito. I found them on the bar in *El Gran Gaitero*."

"They might be fine spectacles, but you can't see with them."

"Oh, but think, Benito, think. Once they might have belonged to a lawyer, or to a doctor, or to a—"

"—to a pimp," Benito snapped, and leaving the bus to its fate, stalked off across the yard, wondering what could be keeping Don Miguel and the buyer.

At the door to the barn he paused to watch Engracia chewing a mouthful of grass and alfalfa, wondering if her placid expression could be taken to mean she liked her fancy new rain hat. Then he continued inside to find José spreading straw and, beside him, María del Carmen shaking and folding blankets. They work well together, he thought, and felt a sudden pang of sadness, for next week José would be in Madrid and María in Amor Milagroso. Benito shook his head, wondering how a man could prefer a noisy, smelly city to the hills and valleys of his native province. And how a girl could let a man in her bed, then not insist that he marry her. Young people, free to pick and choose. What was this nation coming to?

•

At a row of Lombardy poplars the Ferrari turned sharply right and started up the narrow, stony road that led to the Peralta farm and a half-dozen others.

"Hey, everybody, look at that sign," cried Iris, and bracelets ajingle, pointed to a hand-lettered placard nailed to a tree trunk. "The arrow I can understand," she said, "but the rest . . . two years of high school Spanish and I can't read a word."

"Maybe because it's written in *gallego,*" said Don Miguel. "Permit me to translate. The sign says 'This Way to the Celtic Lovers,' and from the number of people along this road, I'd say everyone in the province is taking him up on it."

"You were a fool, letting him keep those statues," Erik muttered.

"What was I supposed to do?" the nobleman asked. "Hire someone to steal them away from him?"

"It's been done."

"Not by me, it hasn't. Besides, you forget. Until yesterday afternoon I was sitting in Monte Carlo, waiting for a certain Danish friend to fly south and join me."

"I told you. I couldn't get away."

"Then don't complain because he's turned this into a bloody carnival!"

"It *is* like a carnival," chirped Iris. "I never saw so many decorated oxcarts. But God, don't these women ever wear anything but black?"

"How can they?" Gabrielle asked sadly. "What with poverty and disease, they're forever mourning a departed loved one."

"Come on, Gaby," pleaded her aunt. "You promised on this vacation you weren't going to talk like that."

"I agreed to the vacation, Aunt Iris. I never said I'd—"

Gabrielle stopped short as the Ferrari wheeled left,

plunged through an opening in the wall, bounced into a barnyard, and screeched to a stop, scattering a crowd of terrified people.

"Hey, is this ever picturesque," Iris exclaimed. "And oh, Erik, look at all those booths. Maybe I can buy something for our exhibit."

"Who's that waving his arms and jumping up and down?" Erik asked. "Is that your farmer?"

"God, no, that's Paco Camino," said Don Miguel. "What's he doing directing traffic? The idiot can barely see." He rolled down his window. "*Oye,* Paco, what's going on? And where's Benito?"

"*Buenas tardes,* Don Miguel," cooed Paco, squinting first at Erik, then at the women behind him. "If your grace would conduct his vehicle to a space we've reserved under the apple tree . . ."

"He's pointing to a soggy piece of canvas," cried Erik. "That's all there is, a soggy piece of canvas."

"Stupid peasants," grumbled Don Miguel, putting the Ferrari in gear. "Still, better a piece of canvas than . . . well, in a barnyard, one never knows."

Benito stood on the doorstep and watched the foursome make their way toward the house. The tall man in the stylish gray suit must be the buyer, he decided. And the brunette in the short blue coat could easily be his wife. But who was the redhead in the tight green dress? She seemed too young to be his mother. An aunt, perhaps. Or maybe somebody's sister.

"Ah, Don Miguel, *buenas tardes,*" Benito called out, his eyes darting from the nobleman's frowning face to the redhead's magnificent bosom. "How pleased I am you and your—"

"All right, Benito," said Don Miguel. "What have you done? Advertised on television? I've been dodging peasants and oxcarts all the way from the village."

"That's because it's the last day, your grace. Even those who have been here before have returned for a final blessing."

"A final what?"

"That's what they call it, your grace. No doubt because it makes them feel good."

"Listen, Benito, we never agreed you could—" He stopped as the redhead touched him on the forearm. "Oh, yes, forgive me. Señora Duveaux, may I present to you Benito Bazán."

"*Mucho gusto,*" she murmured, fluttering her long black lashes.

"*Encantado,*" said Benito, and forced his eyes from her body in time to grasp the extended hand of the woman next to her.

"Señora Van der Linden," said Don Miguel, and as Benito acknowledged the introduction, heard the woman say in fluent Castilian how happy she was to be in Spain and have a chance to visit such a beautiful Galician farm.

"*Gracias.* The señora is from France?"

"No, the United States. Bryn Mawr, Pennsylvania, to be exact."

"Ah, *sí.*" Without the slightest idea where that might be.

"My aunt's from there, too," she added, nodding at the smiling redhead. "But her husband came from France. Her former husband, that is. Right now, Aunt Iris is divorced and living in London."

Benito swallowed his shock. "Ah, *sí.* A very beautiful city, London."

"You know it?"

"Not personally, señora."

"All right, Benito," Don Miguel broke in. "I want you to meet my friend Erik Frostmann."

Frostmann? So the young brunette wasn't his wife. Did that mean she was a divorced woman, too?

"*Mucho gusto,* señor," Benito said, examining the lean, bony face. "I hope you had a pleasant trip and that—"

"*Cinco centavos! Cinco centavos* for the widows and orphans," chanted Teresa León and for emphasis rattled the coins in a wooden cigar box.

Benito dropped the foreigner's hand and hurried over to the doorway. "No, Teresa," he whispered. "Not this group."

"And why not? Are they not more able to give than anybody else?"

"Assuredly, but that's not the point. The point is, Don Miguel and his friends are my guests."

Teresa snorted but stood quietly to one side as Benito urged the foursome to enter the house and consider it their own.

"My God, there are even more people in here!" cried Don Miguel as his eyes moved from the pilgrims lined up against one wall to a group sitting around the table, eating.

"I'm sorry, your grace," Benito said. "They all came at once. On the bus from Las Palomillas."

"We had agreed on secrecy, had we not?"

"Yes, your grace, but with the mayor threatening to—"

"Didn't I tell your wife, the mayor would be taken care of?"

"Yes, your grace. But you see, there was also the problem of El Chavo."

"You mean you— Listen, Benito," he said, lowering his voice, "not a word about that outlaw to Señor Frostmann."

"No, your grace." Wondering what Don Miguel was

going to do when El Chavo and his men came bursting through the door.

"All right," the nobleman said. "Now where are the statues?"

"In there, your grace." Nodding to the doors to the living room.

"Surely you don't expect us to stand in line."

"Of course not, your grace. Perhaps while we wait for the group to leave, you and your friends would enjoy a bowl of stew."

"Stew! Benito, I'm warning you. Get those people out of that room before I—"

"Yes, your grace." And, clenching his fists, turned on his heel and strode to the living room.

As usual the drapes had been drawn and candles flickered in wall sconce and candlestick. Struck by the almost palpable feeling of reverence, Benito drew in his breath and willed himself to become calm. Then, nodding to Andrés Rabal and Manuel Piedra, whose day it was to stand guard inside the double doors, he hurried to the head of the line, rounded the velvet-draped table, and surprised even himself by reaching for Concepción's hand.

"They're here," he croaked, and stared mutely down at the gleaming lovemakers.

"Ay, Benito, is there nothing we can do?"

"Nothing," he breathed. "I gave Don Miguel my word."

Sick at heart, he raised his eyes to the two pilgrims facing him across the table: a man about forty with slumping shoulders and haunted eyes; a woman in her early twenties, so shy she could barely glance at the interlocked twosome before blushing profusely and gaping down at the floor.

"They're Celtic," Benito said softly. "Six hundred years

before the birth of our Lord. And look. They come apart."

"Ay, *qué maravilla!*" gasped the man.

The woman looked up, blushed, turned away.

"You may touch them if you like," Concepción whispered.

The woman stiffened, but the man reached out and stroked the female's smooth, arched belly.

"They're truly beautiful, aren't they?" Concepción persisted.

The woman swallowed; then, raising her eyes, placed a quivering finger on the little man's forearm. "Ay, he's alive," she cried, and grabbed instinctively for the hand of her companion.

"*Gracias. Muchas gracias,*" the man mumbled, and putting his free hand on the woman's waist, guided her away from the table.

Benito watched them go, then raised his palms to the advancing line of pilgrims. "Friends," he called, "it pains me to announce the buyer has arrived and . . ."

And what? Fifty people would have to go home without getting what they came for?

". . . and there will now be a brief intermission," he continued. "Meanwhile, there's food and drink, and I give you my word: before the statues are taken away, everyone here will have a chance to receive the blessing."

"Magnificent. Truly magnificent," sighed Gabrielle Van der Linden.

"*Me gustan mucho,*" said Iris Duveaux. Looked straight at Benito and winked.

"I'm glad my statues have brought the señora pleasure," he said stiffly, then bowed and turned his attention to the men. Don Miguel was stroking his beard and seemed lost in thought; Erik Frostmann, arms folded across his chest, was gazing at the figures with an air of amused contempt.

With sagging spirits, Benito turned back to the women, who in simple Spanish were commenting on this and that feature of the lovers' anatomies. Annoyed, he moved closer to Concepción.

"How is a man to bargain in the presence of so many chattering females?" he whispered.

Concepción shrugged. "They're enjoying what they see. What harm is there in that?"

"You know the temperament of Don Miguel."

"*Sí.*"

"Well, it strikes me Señor Frostmann may have the same inclination."

"So?"

"Don't infuriate me, woman. You know what I'm saying. That the room be cleared of any disturbing influence."

Concepción sniffed and darted a glance at the buxom redhead.

"Listen, *mujer,* must I tell you the real reason I want you and these women out of here? Have you forgotten who else might be attending the sale of these golden statues, how seizing a hostage or two might—"

"Ay, Benito, no! Let me bring back Andrés and Manuel."

"I said no disturbing influence."

And before she could protest, suggested in a loud voice that while the men discussed business, the women relax with a glass of wine. Or, weather permitting, tour the booths and examine some Galician handicrafts.

"Good work, Benito," sighed Don Miguel as a few minutes later the doors closed with a mildly reproving bang. "Women make me nervous. You, too, Erik?"

"I can take them or leave them."

"Ah, yes," said Benito. "And now, perhaps Señor Frostmann would like to examine the figures more carefully."

The blond shrugged but picked up the interlocked pair and turned them this way and that.

"Is the gentleman aware the figures come apart?"

"Yes. Miguel told me."

"*Bueno*, and what is Señor Frostmann's opinion?"

"Very nice . . . if one considers the gold and ignores the ridiculous acrobatics," he said in crisp, slightly accented Castilian.

Spirits lower than ever, Benito edged closer to Don Miguel. "Your friend, señor . . . I fear he doesn't find the statues attractive."

"You mean that comment? That's just his way."

"Then he's still going to buy."

"Buy? Erik isn't a buyer."

"Not a buyer!" Benito couldn't believe his own words.

"Of course not. He's here to appraise the pieces for somebody else."

"Who?"

"How do I know whose bid will be the highest? Erik knows collectors all over Europe."

"But your grace said . . ."

What? What had Don Miguel said so many days ago?

"I told you I'd bring an expert to your farm on the tenth of July."

"Yes, but—"

"Don't look so stunned," Don Miguel said irritably. "Do you think buyers travel to remote corners of the world, their pockets stuffed full of foreign currency?"

Benito hadn't the slightest idea what buyers did. Nor did

he know anything about experts. All he knew was that El Chavo and the mayor wanted those golden figures and this was the last day his friends had agreed to remain on guard.

"I'm sorry, your grace, time is of great importance," Benito said firmly. "Either your friend buys the statues today or our agreement is ended."

"Have you gone crazy, Bazán? What do you mean our agreement is ended?"

"Is something wrong?" Erik asked, setting the interlocked pair back on the table. "Miguel, your face is the color of an overripe tomato."

"Maybe you won't laugh so hard when this peasant tells you what he just told me."

"Ah, and what is that?"

Benito squared his shoulders. "I reminded Don Miguel that according to our agreement these statues were to be sold to his friend on the tenth of July. Today is the tenth, and if the friend of Don Miguel chooses not to buy . . ."

"Listen, Benito, you put those statues on the open market," said Don Miguel, "and you'll be breaking your word of honor. Or isn't that important to people like you?"

"Honor is what the Bazán family lives by," Benito declared, his temples pulsing with anger. "Let Señor Frostmann offer a fair price and the statues are his."

"He'll offer a fair price. But not today."

"Today or never," Benito said, wondering at the source of his stubbornness.

"You strike a hard bargain," said Erik Frostmann. "Yet on the off-chance my friend painted a misleading picture . . ."

"For God's sake, Erik," cried Don Miguel, "whose side are you on?"

"People can make mistakes," Erik replied. "Say one thing. Think they said another."

"People can also hear wrong," the nobleman muttered.

"True," the blond man agreed, "but not having been there . . ." He turned to Benito. "You say time is important. Very well. Thirty days from today I'll be back with an offer and a deposit."

"I'm sorry, señor. Too many people are trying to take these statues away from me."

"Good heavens, Bazán," said Don Miguel. "I have a perfectly good safe up at the villa."

"And I, your grace, have an equally good safe here on the farm."

Don Miguel glanced at the cast-iron box chained to the dentist's chair. "Ha. With the proper tools those links could be severed in an instant."

"All right, I'll compromise again," said Erik Frostmann. "Fifteen days."

"I'm sorry, señor."

"Stupid peasant!" cried Don Miguel. "You know what the problem is, Erik? He's hewing to the foot of the letter. He thinks I told him I'd bring a buyer, so that's what he's determined to meet: a buyer."

"Then I'll compromise a third time," Erik sighed. "In fifteen days—let's see, that'll be on the twenty-fifth of July—I'll bring the deposit, I'll bring the buyer. My God, what more do you expect?"

What more, Benito thought. Some sign you like the golden lovers and will look on them, if not with reverence, at least with affection. *Por Dios,* even an outlaw like El Chavo could be expected to do that.

"I kept my part of the bargain, señores," Benito insisted. "Today is the tenth. There are the statues."

"I intend keeping my part of the bargain, too," the blond declared. "My buyer and I will be here on the twenty-fifth."

"By the twenty-fifth, the statues will be sold." But to whom? Mother of God, he was right back where he'd started.

Maybe he ought to give in. What, after all, were fifteen more days? Ah, but then it would be fifteen more and fifteen more, and the lovers would still end up with some smirking foreigner who considered them ridiculous.

"I hope for your sake those figures will be here when I return," Erik said coldly. "The buyer I have in mind has an extremely hot temper."

"Is that a threat, señor?"

"Take it any way you like."

Don Miguel smiled. "Believe me, Benito, the friends of Erik Frostmann have ways of getting what they want. I know. I've seen some of them in action."

"And that was only a trifling gambling debt," the blond smiled back.

Benito shrugged. "As I said before, señores, today or never. Now if you'll excuse me, I promised the citizens of Las Palomillas they'd have a chance to receive the blessing."

# chapter 20

Engracia stepped on a twig, and at the sudden noise Concepción almost jumped into the pig trough. As she'd almost done when the burro brayed and a chicken made a sudden lunge for a piece of corn. This can't go on, she told herself. Better to feel El Chavo's knife at her throat than live in constant fear he was about to leap out at her from the shrubbery.

Still a bit shaky, she put down her bucket of slops, and noticing Engracia's rain hat was askew, walked over to straighten it. Poor old cow. So many services she performed for a few kind words and a continuing supply of grass and alfalfa. This very minute, now, before lunch, Concepción would go down to the field, and for a change of diet, cut her some corn leaves.

Quickly she strode to the barn and was just picking up her sickle when a car roared into the barnyard. Dropping the tool, she hurried to the door to find Don Miguel's low white car stopping under the apple tree. She caught her breath, then sighed with relief when out stepped not Don Miguel and his friend but Señora Duveaux and Señora Van der Linden.

Now what did they want, she wondered, and started across the yard, determined not to say a word about Benito and José leaving tomorrow for Madrid.

"Hi, I hope we're not intruding," called the brunette, "but my aunt wants to buy some of those pots and baskets she was looking at yesterday."

"*Qué lástima,* señora, the craftsmen are working today in the central market."

"Oh, no. You mean we'll have to buy the things down there?"

Concepción hesitated, knowing that although the craftsmen were gone, much of their work was still in the house. Knowing, too, that when Benito ended the meeting with his guards, the last people he'd want to see would be these companions of Erik Frostmann. Still, if Concepción refused to sell the crafts, wouldn't she, in effect, be stealing bread from the mouths of the craftsmen's children?

"Fortunately, señora, the artisans have left samples of their work," she said at last. "So if the señora and her aunt will precede me into the house . . ."

"Please . . ." The younger woman laid a hand on Concepción's forearm. "I'm Gabrielle, and my aunt's name is Iris."

Concepción's gaze moved from the anxious green eyes to the trim jacket, the wool skirt, the low-heeled leather shoes.

"As the señora wishes," she murmured, and with a sweeping gesture, invited them again to enter the house.

Inside, a murmur of voices came from behind the closed doors of the living room. Breathing a silent prayer that the meeting would last long enough for the women to finish their business and leave, Concepción led them to a trestle table on which stood a random assortment of pots, baskets, carvings, clothing, and jewelry.

"Oh, how wonderful," gushed the redhead, and scooping up a finely woven tray, carried it to the window to examine it in the light.

For a few moments Gabrielle watched her aunt in silence, then, taking Concepción by the arm, moved her farther along the wall.

"Is Benito here?" she whispered. "I've got a letter for him from Don Diego."

"Ay, *mi madre!*"

"Is that something to be afraid of?"

"I don't know, señora—"

"Gabrielle."

"—Doña Gabriela. No one in Amor Milagroso has ever received such a thing."

"Maybe that's why the duke asked me to keep it quiet. I thought it was because it had something to do with the statues and Erik Frostmann. My aunt works for him, you know."

"No, Doña Gabriela, I didn't," murmured Concepción, slipping the letter inside the V of her blouse.

"Mmmm, well, Erik owns an art gallery up in London, and my aunt helps him set up the exhibits. That's what she's doing now. Collecting things for a show she's going to call 'Folk Art of Galicia.' Though considering how this trip has worked out, why Erik would want such a thing completely escapes me."

"You like him, this man?" Concepción asked softly.

"What a strange thing to ask." Gabrielle looked at her quizzically; then, as if making up her mind about something, said, "Beware of Erik Frostmann, Concepción. My aunt doesn't say much, but from what I saw and heard last night at the villa . . ."

She stopped. Looked nervously over her shoulder. "I love those golden figures, Concepción, and I'd hate to see Erik Frostmann take them away from you."

"*Por Dios,* señora, are you suggesting that Señor Frostmann is a thief?"

"Who knows? All over Europe there are men who steal to order from villas, museums, even cathedrals. Whether Erik knows such men or buys what they steal or even steals a few choice items himself, who's to say? I only hope you and your husband own a good, solid safe."

Concepción smiled. "At night the lovers sleep in a place no thief would ever dream existed."

"These thieves are different. I read where . . ."

She turned away as the doors to the living room burst open

and out stalked Benito, followed by Paco Camino and three scowling men from the village.

"One hour, that's all we're asking," the first man cried.

"Considering all we've done, I think you at least owe us that," the second man put in.

"Of course, of course," Benito agreed, rounding the central table. "But now that I'm no longer protected by Don Miguel, what's to stop the mayor from sending fifty men? Putting us all in jail? And then there's El Chavo. Don't forget about El Chavo."

"Four o'clock," the third man called out, stalking to the door. "I'll have Eliseo bring out every chair and table in the place."

"It's useless," Benito called after him. "Useless. How can farmers and fishermen possibly—"

He froze, his eyes focused on Iris Duveaux as she came toddling from the window on high-heeled satin shoes.

"*Buenas tardes,* Señor Bazán," she chirped. "I'm finding so many pretty things here. Look. Isn't this precious?"

She held out a small carved fishing boat complete with sails, nets, floats, and anchor. "And that!" Pointing to a green satin wall hanging. "*Vivan los célticos,*" she read dramatically. Then giggled. "Even I know what that means."

"War," Benito said flatly.

"What?"

"The señora has just uttered our village war cry."

Puzzled, the redhead turned to her niece for a translation. Meanwhile, Concepción hurried to her husband's side and quickly told him why Iris was there and, more important, whom she worked for.

"All right, all right," Benito muttered. "Just get them out of here."

Which Concepción proceeded to do, then asked Benito to load the crafts in the trunk of the car. He was just finishing when José and María entered the yard with a burro laden with foodstuffs.

"Bad news, *papá,*" the young man called out. "The Gypsies are camping in the fields of Enrique Patino."

"Oooohhhh, Gypsies," cooed Iris. "How romantic."

"Not for one who, like our neighbor Enrique, has fine horses and a good milk cow," Benito said sternly.

"Ay, José! See to Engracia!" Concepción gasped.

"*Mamá,* not even a Gypsy would steal a cow like Engracia."

"Do as your mother says," Benito barked. "And until those Gypsies go, that cow will live in the laundry shed."

"These Gypsies," Gabrielle put in, "do they come here often?"

"Unfortunately yes," Benito sighed. "Every year . . . just before the *Romería.*"

"Ah, the *Romería,*" said Iris. "*Muy gran fiesta, verdad?* Many flags. Many flowers. Many men in, ah, special black hats."

"Oh, Aunt Iris," Gabrielle said impatiently. "Those men were in the *Guardia Civil.*"

"What's that?"

"Ask them." Nodding at the Bazáns.

"So the *Guardia*'s in Amor Milagroso," Benito said thoughtfully.

"Three truckloads," said Gabrielle. "Does that mean trouble?"

"Not for you, señora."

"And for you?"

"The señora has many questions."

"I'm sorry. Force of habit. Come on, Aunt Iris, let's be on our way so these people can get back to work."

The redhead bade them *hasta luego* and climbed in the car; but, hand on the door latch, her companion paused, then beckoned to Concepción.

"Perhaps I shouldn't say this," she whispered, "but Erik Frostmann isn't the only one eager to get his hands on those little figures. Last night after dinner, your mayor . . . Pablo Estrada, is that his name?"

"*Sí,* señora, Pablo Estrada."

"Quite a charming man, by the way. And he writes such sensitive lyric poetry. Hard to believe he's—what? Fifty? Fifty-five?"

"Don Pablo took office at twenty-three. Just before Galicia fell to the *Generalísimo.*"

"So that would make him . . . my God, somewhere in his sixties!"

"Don't be discouraged, señora. The uncle of Eliseo Rabal married again when he was seventy."

"Oh, but I wasn't thinking of—"

"Gaby, what's going on?" Iris shouted from inside the car.

"Nothing!" Gabrielle shouted back, her face red with embarrassment. "Yes, well, all I wanted to say . . . your mayor is making plans to put those statues in a museum."

"Thank you, señora. This news does not surprise me."

"Oh. Well, if there's anything I can do to help you fight for your rights . . ."

A tremor of fear raced down Concepción's backbone. "We're not thinking of fighting, señora."

"Oh, but you have to. Otherwise people like Erik and Miguel are going to walk all over you."

"Gaby, hurry up!"

"Four o'clock at the café, right?" And before Concepción could protest, the young woman climbed in the car, started up the motor, and drove off.

# chapter 21 🌺🌺🌺

Never—not even at the height of the *Romería*—had *El Gran Gaitero* held so many people. Every chair, every bench, every centimeter of space in front of the windows and along the dark, wainscoted walls was occupied by a man or woman from Amor Milagroso.

Leaning against the bar, Benito scanned the sea of faces. Concepción. Manolo and his wife, Angela. Señora Duveaux and Señora Van der Linden. Ignacio and Teresa León. Enrique Patino. Victoria Montalvo. Andrés Rabal. Manuel Piedra. Tío Arturo. Tía Rosa. Even that scowling young man, Pedro Pérez, surrounded by four equally grim-faced young friends.

"Ay, Benito," whispered Paco, turning from the crowd to pick up his wineglass. "Does not the presence of so many people make you long for the simple life of a fisherman?"

"Nowadays there's no such thing," Benito said sadly. "One can't be a simple anything. Not even the simple owner of a pair of statues."

"Then perhaps it's just as well I sold *La Mariposa*. Though in truth, I miss her greatly."

140

"So do I, *viejo*. So do I."

"But you have your treasure. That has brought you great happiness, has it not?"

"And also great worries. Not the least of which is what to say to this roomful of individuals."

Groaning softly, he thrust his hands in his pockets, where his right hand curled around the letter from Don Diego. At the moment, it was tempting to do what that letter proposed, if only for the pleasure of seeing what would happen when one Granflaqueza was pitted against another. Ay, but that was only a daydream. Never would Benito do business with the man everyone held responsible for the death of Benito's father.

"It's half-past four," whispered Paco. "Don't you think it's time to begin?"

"Just what I was about to do," Benito said, and rapped on the bar. The noise level dropped, and heads swiveled toward him expectantly.

"Friends and fellow citizens . . ."

"We know who we are," barked Tío Arturo. "Say what you have to say and be done with it."

"You already know what I have to say," Benito barked back. "Namely, that my statues haven't been sold, and before I take them elsewhere, some of my friends insisted I speak to you about selling them here. Which I maintain is impossible. Who in a roomful of farmers and fishermen could possibly introduce me to anyone rich enough to buy a treasure? Ah, said my friends, if only one person knows one person, your troubles are over."

"If I knew such a person, I'd ask him to buy me a new roof," a male voice hollered.

"Or a stronger mast," yelled somebody else.

"Another burro."

"A week in Marseilles!"

"I don't understand why he has to sell the statues at all," said César Soto, Amor Milagroso's aging, half-blind dentist. "Why can't he just keep them on display and charge admission?"

"Because my husband and his friends are tired of serving as watchdogs," snapped Teresa León.

"Benito," cried Victoria Montalvo, waving for his attention. "How many pesetas would a buyer have to have? More than a thousand?"

"More than a hundred thousand," Benito said proudly.

"And if you never find anyone to buy them?" Eliseo called from behind the bar. "What happens then?"

"Such a possibility never occurred to me," Benito said stiffly. "There's bound to be a buyer somewhere. That's why tomorrow morning . . ."

He hesitated, thinking, why let all these people, above all the friends of Erik Frostmann, know he was leaving tomorrow for Madrid. Who knows, they might try to stop him.

"Tomorrow morning what?" a farmer insisted.

"The statues go back on display," a fisherman answered.

"No, wait," Benito shouted. "I never said—"

"We have to let people know," a woman cried from over near the windows.

"How?" another woman asked from across the room.

"Letter more placards," someone suggested.

"Hang them all over town."

"And put some on the bus to Las Palomillas."

"And Pontevedra."

"La Coruña."

"Send them to every city along the coast."

"And inland."

"To other provinces."

"Wait!" Benito hollered. "Those statues are mine! I'm going to—"

"Does everyone know Teresa collected six hundred pesetas for the widows and orphans?" Ignacio interrupted.

"And my son Guillermo sold thirty-three banners reading *Vivan los célticos,*" shouted a woman next to him.

"*Vivan los célticos!*" cried Pedro Pérez.

"*Vivan los célticos!*" echoed the crowd.

Eliseo pounded on the bar. "I've just had a magnificent idea. Let's include the statues in the *Romería* procession."

"*Sí, sí,*" the crowd agreed.

"Bring the lovers to the *Romería* grounds."

"*UN MOMENTO!*" a familiar voice boomed out, and every face turned toward the doorway. "First the war cry, now the manifesto," shouted Pablo Estrada as six *Guardias* filed past him into the room. "Just as I thought, this is a meeting for anarchists and revolutionaries."

"It's time to leave," Manuel Piedra called out as a *Guardia* stopped beside his table. "The *Maria Elena* is tugging at her lines."

"And the udders of my cow are strained to the bursting point."

"The grass in my pasture is halfway to my knees."

"Who will walk with me to the market?"

"Wait! Come back!" cried Pablo Estrada. "I was about to declare this meeting disbanded."

"Too late, Don Pablo," said Eliseo Rabal. "I'd say the anarchists and revolutionaries have disbanded it for you."

# chapter 22

The afternoon sun was painting the world a luminous gold as the Porsche, with Iris Duveaux at the wheel, pulled away from the café and embarked on a thunderous course through the narrow, winding streets of the village. Not that Benito noticed either the light or the warmth, or cared about them one way or the other. All that concerned him was escaping the mayor and getting back to the farm. Something was wrong up there; he could feel it.

"Your wife," said Iris, gripping the wheel as though to squeeze out the proper Spanish words, "I thought for a moment she wasn't going to permit you to come with me."

"My wife doesn't command. Not in my house," Benito declared. But he'd been aware of Concepción's narrowed eyes when he'd accepted the redhead's invitation. And that was before Señora Van der Linden had decided to get out of the car and talk with Pablo Estrada.

"You spoke well this afternoon," Iris announced as the car picked up speed on the road outside of town.

"Thank you, señora." Thinking, too bad his audience hadn't agreed to listen.

"*Por nada,*" she said, and shifted her shoulders so those magnificent breasts swelled against the cotton of her blouse.

Ill at ease alone with such a voluptuous and exotic female, Benito turned to his window, wondering how long it was going to take to get home. Surely, he'd arrive hours earlier than he would have if he'd ridden the burro. So it was good he'd accepted Señora Duveaux's offer. Besides, his going back to guard the statues meant Concepción could stay as long as she liked with Manolo and his wife, Angela. In truth, Benito would have enjoyed visiting his son's house, too. But there wasn't time. There wasn't time for anything anymore. Talking with his sons, sitting in the café, drinking more than was good for him . . .

"I wonder what's happening with my niece and Pablo Estrada," Iris said as the Porsche swerved around an oxcart.

"Happening, señora?"

"You know . . ." She smiled coyly, and Benito stiffened. Was she suggesting that the aging mayor and the beautiful young woman were doing more than just discussing the meeting? Impossible. The brunette wasn't that flighty. And Pablo Estrada was far too decrepit.

"I don't know, señora," Benito replied. "The mayor and I are not what one would call friends."

"But men are men, *verdad?*"

"To a certain point . . ." Again he turned to his window. Was it his imagination, or were the fields and trees flashing by more slowly?

"Is there some problem with the motor, señora?"

Iris grinned and fluffed her hair with an accompanying jangle of bracelets. "It's such a beautiful afternoon. Why hurry?"

"I'm worried about the farm, señora. I didn't leave many guards because—" He stopped, remembering who Señora Duveaux worked for.

"Don't worry," she laughed, "we'll be there before— Look. What's that over there?"

She pointed to a meadow where plumes of smoke rose from

behind a dozen covered wagons grouped in a semicircle.

"Bah. That's the encampment of the Gypsies."

"Ooohh, wonderful," she cooed, and stepping hard on the brakes, pulled onto the grass that bordered the roadway. "I want to see them," she declared.

"Please, señora."

"What's the matter? Isn't it safe?"

"If one has no money, no jewelry . . ."

"I'll take it off. Look," she said, and grinning like a mischievous child, pulled off a diamond ring, dangle earrings, and six metal bracelets, dropped them into her purse, and snapped the catch.

"But the farm," he protested. "If anything goes wrong, my son—"

"Five minutes." She stepped out onto the road and shaded her eyes. "This looks fantastic. Wait. Where's my camera?"

She rummaged in the rear seat; then, camera around her neck, set off across the field in her high-heeled wedgies. Benito groaned. Such stupidity. Wasting valuable time on thieves and horse-traders. Still, he couldn't let the woman visit the camp alone, he decided. So, muttering under his breath, he got out of the car and hurried after her.

"Oh, this is marvelous," Iris crooned, aiming her lens at the dirty, naked children who came swarming out to greet them. Then, laughing and chattering, she snapped the porch of one of the wagons, six dead rats hanging by their hind legs from a rope stretched between two trees, a mangy yellow dog, and a wrinkled old woman who came hobbling over from one of the campfires.

"One peseta," she whined, rubbing her fingers together. "One peseta for a drink of wine."

"Go to the devil," Benito muttered, his nostrils twitching at the woman's foul smell.

"How picturesque," Iris cried. "And look. That one's even better."

She turned her lens to a girl of sixteen in a loose blouse and long skirt who was walking toward them with a naked baby astride her hip. Right away the crone grabbed Iris's elbow.

"Three pesetas, three pesetas," she chanted.

"Here," Benito snapped, and handed her some coins, together with instructions to get back to her cooking and leave the lady in peace. The crone shambled away, and Benito nudged aside the mangy yellow dog and headed for the shade of a nearby oak tree. There he stood sullen and resentful, smoking a cigarette while Iris tottered around the camp taking pictures of horses, wagons, urchins, and dogs until more and more women left off stirring their pots, more and more men got up from their naps, and she was encircled by pushing, shouting people holding their hands out.

Time to go, he decided, and holding tight to his money, hurried forward and told her so.

"But this lady's going to tell my fortune," Iris protested, nodding at the crone, who'd again left her caldron and was grinning at him from behind Iris's back.

"That would be most unwise," Benito said, and taking hold of the redhead's arm, guided her gently but firmly across the meadow to the car.

"It's so warm," Iris complained, hand on the door latch. "If only . . . yes, look over there." She pointed to a tree-shaded brook on the far side of the road.

"Señora, please, I beg of you . . ."

"Three minutes," she cried, running across the pavement.

God in heaven, what was a man to do with such an exasperating female? Flushed with anger, Benito followed her across the road, down the slope, and along the stream to a place where Iris could stoop down and dip her fingers in the clear, cool water.

"Oh, how marvelous," she sighed, moistening her cheeks, throat, and the crevice between her breasts. Then, rising to her feet, she opened her purse and handed him a small silver flask. "*Agua caliente,*" she grinned.

He hesitated, then thought, why not? Whiskey might give him the courage he needed to start home on foot and leave Señora Duveaux to the Gypsies.

"What a man," she murmured as he handed the flask back to her. "You're very handsome right now, Benito Bazán."

He smiled and took a nervous step backward.

"Poor Benito," she laughed. Then tipped her head and drank some of the liquor herself. "Mmmmm. This is good. I think I'm going to stay here forever."

So saying, she sank to some grass at the base of a maple tree. "*Agua caliente, agua caliente,*" she chanted, raising the flask and waving it gaily. "You don't want anymore? Then it's all for me. *Vivan los célticos!*"

*Por Dios,* what a capacity for alcohol, Benito thought as his eyes slid down her throat, over her breasts and belly, then down her skirt to her plump bare legs. Suddenly a familiar bulge distended his old black trousers. Mother of God, he thought, at this point even José would know enough to turn on his heel and race to the roadway.

"Sit down, sit down," the redhead urged, patting the grass next to her.

He hesitated. Licked his lips. "One minute, not a second more."

Iris grinned and handed him the flask. This is ridiculous, he thought as the burning liquid trickled down his throat. I should get up. Run to the farm. Anything.

He wiped his lips and offered the flask to the woman, but Iris was lying down with her eyes closed and her hands behind her head. And her skirt, he noticed, was halfway up her thigh. Swallowing dryly, he reached forward and touched the soft, warm flesh.

"Ay, Benito, Benito," she moaned, and moved her legs apart.

Benito gaped at her in awe. Did she really . . . ? Here . . . ?

Putting down the flask, he got clumsily to his knees. Across the road a horse whinnied and a dog began to bark. He looked around. The woodland was shadowy and silent. And the woman . . . ay, how ripe and lovely. And how much she wanted it. By heaven, there were times a man had a responsibility!

With fumbling fingers he unbuttoned his trousers.

Iris twitched. "Hurry, Benito. Hurry."

He reached inside his pants. Froze as a sound from the outside world entered his consciousness.

He raised his eyes. Saw in the bushes a dozen dark-skinned children fixing him with their evil, mocking eyes.

Though at first he'd cursed the giggling urchins, by the time the Porsche neared the turnoff to the farm, Benito was thanking them mentally for having saved him not only from sin but from what certainly would have been an unbearably guilty conscience. As it was, he might feel like a fool, but he could look his wife straight in the eye. Though not the redhead. But judging from the silence in the car, and the way the tires squealed when she made a U-turn and headed back to the village, in the future Benito Bazán would probably never get close enough to Iris Duveaux to make looking in her eyes a problem.

Which, aside from his pride, didn't bother him in the least, he told himself as he turned from the road into the farmyard. Almost at once, he sensed something was wrong. Everything seemed so quiet. And why had those pigs been given cabbages and potatoes?

"José!" he shouted. "María!"

Except for contented grunts, nothing but silence.

"No," he murmured, "no," and in a panic ran to the house and opened the door. In the main room, chairs had been over-turned, lamps smashed, pictures flung to the floor. Even the insides of an alarm clock had been pulled from the case and tossed into a corner.

Cursing aloud, Benito picked his way through the debris and entered the kitchen. There the story was the same. Broken jugs. Split sacks. Fireplace ashes strewn over everything. And on José's cot, the mattress slashed, the sheets and blankets ripped.

Sickened by what he'd seen, terrified by the thought of what might yet await his eyes, Benito stumbled to the living-room doors and yanked them open. Disaster. Chaos. But, merciful God, no dead bodies.

Quickly he passed the overturned chairs, the uprooted plants, and stopped before the ancient dentist's chair. Chained to its arms was the cast-iron box, its lock smashed, its top wrenched open. Empty of all but its cotton nest, the box told him nothing. Nor did the carved wooden box lying splintered at his feet.

Tears welled in his eyes at the thought of that beautiful work of art beneath the heel of some vindictive bandit. And what had those brutes done to Benito's son?

Gasping for breath, he staggered from the room and out into the yard.

"José! María!"

The barn. Maybe they were in the barn. He dashed to the door. Stopped. Cocked an ear. Something or someone was stirring in a distant corner. He reached for a hoe, a rake—anything. Found the handles of all of his tools had been snapped in two.

"Miserable bastards," he muttered, and picking up the business half of a hoe, hurried forward.

"José?"

There was a rustling noise, followed by moaning. Hoe at the ready, he approached the shadowy corner. Found his six young guards—sons and nephews of the men who'd attended the meeting—bound and gagged, lying in the straw.

"God in heaven," he breathed, dropped to his knees by the nearest boy, pulled the cloth from his mouth, and asked what had happened.

A nightmare, the young man reported, rubbing his wrists as Benito began untying the boy next to him. He'd been watching, as had all the others, but suddenly there they were, six of them, all in black, with ski masks over their faces and machine pistols in their hands, just like on television. There wasn't any fight, not with those men, silent, eerie, encircling the yard, tying them up; then when they finally decided the young men were telling the truth, that they didn't know where the statues were, methodically going about the routine of search and destruction.

"And José?" Benito asked when all the young men were free and each had verified the story of the others.

"The last I saw he was at the laundry shed with María del Carmen," said the nephew of Roberto López.

"God in heaven," Benito cried, and heart pounding, raced to the shed and pulled open the door. Water in the cistern.

Straw on the floor. Grass and alfalfa piled in a corner. And that was that.

Knees weak, Benito leaned against the cold stone wall. So much pain, so much anguish, and for what? A few weeks of anxious daydreaming. Why did he have to chase that fox, crawl through that tunnel? He could have cultivated the Peralta farm for years. Enjoyed the riches he'd already been given. A wife, fine sons . . .

He staggered from the shed and raised his eyes to the oak-crowned hillside. "Was it you who did this, Vicente?" he breathed. "You should have come when you were supposed to. Or later. We could have reached an agreement."

Or I could have gone to you, he thought. Of course. When I didn't sell to Erik Frostmann, I could have gone to you . . .

But I didn't. I don't know why; I just didn't. And now it's too late. Your men have come and robbed me of everything.

Barely able to lift his feet, Benito trudged back to the house and climbed wearily onto the doorstep.

"*Oye, papá!* How was the meeting?"

He wheeled. Gaped at his son, who with María del Carmen at his side and Engracia at his heels was striding toward him across the barnyard.

"Where . . . where have you been?" Benito croaked.

"The cornfield," José answered brightly.

"The cornfield?"

José looked embarrassed. "Since I'm leaving tomorrow, María and I wanted to talk. And you said we had to keep a constant watch over Engracia—"

"—who dearly loves corn leaves," María put in.

"—so that's why we went," José finished. "And if you're angry, *papá*, well, I'm sorry, but that's what happened."

"Angry! *Mi hijo*, you've saved us all," Benito cried, and

jumping from the step, enfolded his son in a breathtaking *abrazo*.

Then, wiping away his tears, Benito walked to the cow and patted the comforting extra weight in her shaggy new rain hat.

# chapter 23

As the Granflaqueza family dominated the people in the village, so the Granflaqueza mansion, Villa Alegre, dominated the rocky bluffs just outside of town. The sprawling country house or *pazo,* as such establishments are called in that part of Spain, dated from Duke Alonso in the fourteenth century, but had been improved, or at least added on to, by every succeeding duke thereafter. Thus, by the twentieth century, the rambling gray stone building had accumulated an astonishing assortment of patios and porticos, balconies and turrets, plus a square stone tower from which one could see the village to the east, the firth directly ahead, an imposing promontory to the west, and rolling hills across the highway to the north. However, should the resident duke tire of overlooking his domain, he had only to come down from his tower, follow a meandering path to the edge of the bluff, descend a hundred and eighteen steps, and he would find himself in a secluded cove which boasted a white sand beach, a long wooden pier, and in previous years, a sleek white sailboat.

Lately, however, both beach and pier were usually deserted, the current duke preferring to spend his days contemplating sea and sky while sipping Scotch and listening to baroque chamber music. Thus, the morning after the attack on the Peralta farm, it was in no way surprising that Diego Granflaqueza, duke of Última Alegría, was sitting in his *mirador* listening to the Vivaldi Concerto in D for flute, strings, and continuo when Benito Bazán, dressed in his only suit and mounted on his only burro, turned from the coastal highway into the driveway leading to the villa. Nor was it surprising that the duke, happening to glance from the window, assumed his letter to Benito had been favorably received and told his housekeeper, Luisa, to open the gate.

As he drew close to the high stone wall, Benito began to have serious misgivings. What was he doing, thinking of selling his treasure to an age-old family enemy? His father, Federico, must be spinning in his grave. Strange how last night, Benito's offering the statues to Don Diego had seemed the wisest, most logical thing to do. In fact during those long, dark hours when Engracia drowsed in the shed and a dozen guards kept watch in the yard, even waiting until morning seemed reckless and inadvisable. But now, in the sunlight, everything seemed different. Surely there must be something else he could do. Go home, for example. Sit down with the family and consider the matter calmly.

Just then the gate creaked open and a woman in black called a brisk *buenos días,* said the duke was expecting him, and asked would he please dismount and follow her to the rear entrance.

Not knowing what else to do, Benito led his burro down the drive, past the tile-roofed portico that protected the entry, along a wall whose arched windows reminded him of a church, around a corner, and across a yard to a nondescript door in what was clearly the service wing. There, the woman nodded to a railing, and Benito hitched up his burro, glancing as he did so across the yard to the garage. The doors were open, and inside an elderly man was polishing a blue Seat parked beside a black Mercedes. What luck, Benito thought, reasoning that since there was no sign of either the Porsche or the Ferrari, Don Miguel and his guests had gone elsewhere.

"In here," the woman called, and before Benito could utter a word, set off down a narrow, dimly lit corridor that led past a large tiled kitchen where a girl sliced onions while an older woman stirred something in a pot, then a pantry whose floor-to-ceiling shelves were stacked high with dishes and glassware. Beyond this room the woman glanced over her shoulder to make sure Benito was still there; then, reaching in her pocket for a key, unlocked the carved wooden door that led to the rest of the manor house. That done, she smoothed down her dress, patted her hair, and strode briskly forward on the red runner that ran down the center of the wide, vaulted passageway.

Ill at ease, Benito set off after her, his eyes roaming from the portraits on his right to the view of pine trees and sea visible through the windows on his left. Suddenly the woman turned sharply right and started down an even broader passage with an even higher ceiling. Here the walls were hung not with paintings but with tapestries, between which stood suits of armor, each seemingly guarding a beautifully carved door.

Just as Benito had begun to wonder if the woman was going to lead him through the entire villa and out the front door, she stopped abruptly and bade him enter a book-lined room with comfortable chairs, an Oriental rug, and, despite its being morning, a crackling fire in a marble fireplace. "Now, you're not to tire him," she declared, and with a disapproving glance at Benito's dusty shoes and thirty-year-old suit, sniffed audibly and started back to the service wing.

Alone, Benito gaped at the books, the flowers, the rosewood desk, the maroon velvet chairs at either side of the fireplace. It was going to be difficult, talking with a man who lived in a place like this. How was Benito going to explain his decision so the duke wouldn't get angry and maybe take action against the Bazáns, or join forces with his son and Señor Frostmann?

He was still considering that problem when he heard footsteps in the hall, and a moment later a small, white-haired man in a suede jacket, patterned scarf, and brown trousers walked through the open doorway.

"Ah, Benito Bazán," he said, gesturing vaguely with a cigarette in a silver holder. "At last you made up your mind to answer my letter."

"*Sí,* señor, but—"

"Sit down, sit down. Would you enjoy a glass of wine, or is it too early in the morning?"

"No, señor. That is, thank you, but it is not my intention—"

"A friend of mine in Jerez sent me a cask of amontillado," Don Diego said as he pulled a braided cord next to the fireplace. "It's quite good, though that story by Poe makes even mentioning it seem ominous."

Benito took a hesitant step forward. "Please, your grace . . ."

"Yes?"

"Excuse me, but I've thought the matter over and, well, I'm sorry, your grace, but—"

"You're selling to somebody else."

Benito sagged with relief. "*Sí,* señor. *Eso es.*"

"Not that namby-pamby friend of my son, I hope."

"No, señor."

"Who, then?"

"I . . . er . . . that is . . ."

"I see." The duke sat down and crushed out his cigarette. "So you still believe those malicious rumors about my family."

"I believe what I have seen, señor."

"And what is that?"

There was a dry cough, and the woman walked in, grave and apologetic. Impatiently, the duke ordered the sherry, and, when the woman left, leaned his white head against the maroon velvet.

"Now. What makes you so convinced my father and I were murderers?"

Benito squared his shoulders. "My father with a bullet in his back. My uncles leaving in the middle of the night for France. My mother dying of grief."

"Truly a terrible series of events. But hardly proof a Granflaqueza was responsible. Especially since my father, too, was killed in the night by an unknown assassin."

"People in the village said Don Eugenio died of a heart attack."

"That was what they were told. Just as they were told—by somebody else, of course—that my father was a Fascist."

Benito frowned, remembering the stern-faced man sitting beside beribboned generals and smiling priests as he toured the village in his black limousine.

"To my eyes, your grace," he said, "Don Eugenio was a friend of everyone in power."

"That's because you saw only appearances, Benito. Unlike your father, who was superbly capable of seeing the truth."

"Which is, señor?"

"That appearances are deceiving. My father, like yours, was killed by the fascists. As was his grandson, my eldest boy, Rodrigo Luis. You didn't know that, did you? You thought, like everybody else, that Don Eugenio died in his bed, and Rodrigo Luis in a sports car near Biarritz."

The duke leaned forward. "Now I'll tell you the truth, Benito Bazán. My father died in a forest near La Coruña. My eldest son in a Basque village, high in the Pyrenees. Thus, both were victims of the war, though in the case of my son the year was nineteen sixty-nine. Do you understand what I'm saying?"

"Your words, señor, are taking on a strange meaning."

"And a dangerous one. Come, let me show you that Benito Bazán and Diego Granflaqueza have more in common than you ever dreamed possible."

Benito raised high the silver candelabrum (the mice having long since eaten the wires that served this part of the mansion), wondering what in this musty old ballroom could make a fisherman feel closer to a duke.

"Now this may look to you like a warehouse," Don Diego said, gesturing toward the walls lined with sheet-covered furniture, "but I swear I've sold so many antiques to finance our cause I feel like the old *hidalgo* in *Lazarillo de Tormes*."

Benito grunted, not having the slightest idea who that gentleman was, and set out with the duke across the creaking wooden floor.

"Some things I'll never sell, though," Don Diego continued. "That, for instance." He pointed to a large portrait hanging above the medieval fireplace. "Yes, there he is: Luis Antonio Granflaqueza y Fuerte Anhelo, founder of our village and of my family."

Benito lifted the candelabrum so the light would fall on Don Luis's face as well as on his scrawny, satin-clad body. What greeted him were glittering eyes, sunken cheeks, and an almost demented smile.

"My noble ancestor," the duke said softly. "A wastrel who ended his days copulating in an oak grove." Then, turning his back on Don Luis, he gestured vaguely at the other three walls. "And there are all the others. Come, let me introduce you."

So saying, he started around the room, encouraging Benito to study well the caballeros, clerics, soldiers, and dandies, plus assorted wives, mothers, sisters, and children who stared at them from ornate gilded frames.

"You may wonder why I wanted you to see this," the duke said as they completed their tour and neared again the door to the central corridor. "It's very simple. I wanted you to know that I, like you, am weighted down by the past. Not because I curse others for having been unjust to my family, but because I curse my family for having been so unjust. With one exception." He stopped before the portrait of a dark-haired man in a suit from the 1920s. "My father—like yours, Benito—was a man of whom any thinking *gallego* could feel proud."

"And I thought he was the same as all the others," Benito murmured. Then realized what he had said. "Ay, your grace," he cried, "forgive me. I only meant—"

"That's all right," Don Diego said with a smile. "How were you to know my father was fighting for the same things yours was? Nobody knew that. Not even my son Miguel."

He shook his head. "So many years, so many unmarked graves. And it's still going on, Benito. That's why I sent you that letter. Not just to encourage you to sell us your golden statues, but to ask your help in . . . *bueno,* let's talk about that back in the library."

Life was strange, Benito thought as he watched Don Diego pour a generous amount of sherry from a cut-glass decanter into each of two cut-glass goblets. Who would have guessed Benito Bazán could ever feel respect for the duke of Última Alegría?

"Now," said Don Diego, handing him a glass, "let's drink to a successful partnership."

Benito hesitated, then realized that since Don Diego hadn't been responsible for Federico's death, there was no reason not to sell him the statues.

He smiled, lifted his glass. "To a worthy home for the golden lovers."

"And a long life for Octavio Mora."

Benito froze. "I'm sorry, señor. I cannot drink to that."

"Ah, my friend. Still deceived by appearances."

"You mean—"

"I mean Octavio and your father could easily have become the closest of friends. Sit down, Benito, and let me tell you why I say this."

Octavio Mora, the duke explained, while supposedly a staunch supporter of General Franco and the ultraconservative, right-wing "bunker," had, since before the war, been fighting behind the scenes for such liberal ideals as universal education, religious freedom, and a blanket amnesty for political prisoners.

"I know that sounds incredible," Don Diego admitted,

"but all I can say is that when a man belongs to one of the noblest families in Castile, people tend to believe he has the same ideas as his ancestors."

Naturally, in the course of Mora's career there were many occasions when his dual role was almost discovered. In the early 1970s, for instance, he'd traveled to Granada and, disguised as a carpenter, attended a meeting of those who believe workers have a right to form unions. The group was attacked by the army and took refuge in the cathedral. Fearful of being captured and recognized, Mora slipped into a chapel, removed his disguise, and strolled behind some tourists to the tomb of Ferdinand and Isabella. From there it was relatively easy to follow the tourists out to the street, proceed past the trucks filled with soldiers, and eventually make his way back to his hotel room.

Lately, however, Mora hadn't been quite so cautious. Maybe because at age seventy-five he was more concerned with getting things done than with keeping up appearances. Or maybe he was just getting tired. Whatever the reason, a few months back he'd made some imprudent remarks in the Cortes, and rumor had it an investigation was now under way.

"If the 'bunker' ever learns of Mora's letters to La Pasionaria or Marcelino Camacho . . ." The duke shook his head. "He'd get thirty years. An ironic fate for a man who has long advocated political amnesty, *verdad?*"

"*Claro,* señor. But what you have told me . . . it's dangerous to speak so freely. For your grace as well as Señor Mora."

"You aren't one to send Mora to his death, Benito. On the contrary, I hope you'll be the one who brings him to freedom."

"I, señor?" A chill ran down Benito's spine, and he raised his glass for a warming gulp of sherry.

"I realize I have no right to assume you'll be willing to join us," the duke said softly, "yet once you hear what we have in mind . . ."

The plan, he said, was simplicity itself. The night of the *Romería*, Don Octavio and his family would say good-bye to the duke, climb in their rented car, and set off to visit friends up in La Coruña. These friends would wait a reasonable length of time, then telephone the authorities. A search would begin, and eventually the rented car would be found at the base of a cliff, ten kilometers from Amor Milagroso. Whoever was driving must have missed a curve on that narrow, winding road, the police would say. And the family? Poor souls. One could only hope their bodies would be returned by the sea . . .

"Yes, it will be quite a tragedy," Don Diego proclaimed, "and also quite a mystery. Not, however, for the one who hired the driver, selected the cliff, arranged for the rowboat on the beach and the fishing boat anchored offshore."

The duke leaned forward. "That boat, Benito, is *La Mariposa*. Her destination, an English yacht cruising in the Atlantic, just beyond the mouth of the firth."

"*La Mariposa*," Benito gasped. "Then it was your grace who . . . señor, are you aware the men who bought that boat almost killed me and Paco Camino?"

The duke sighed and set down his sherry glass. "Paco tripped over a stool while hurrying from his bed to the door. His glasses he knocked from a table and accidentally stepped on."

Benito narrowed his eyes. "And how did these men say Benito Bazán received his bruises?"

"Ah, that was a different situation entirely. Ramón and Pepe thought you'd been hired by the government. Then when the Scarecrow saved your life, they were more convinced than ever. Later, when they told me what had happened . . ."

Shaking his head, the duke reached for a cigarette. "It's clear now I should have met with them more often. But in the beginning it all seemed so simple. Talk to Paco. Buy the boat. Bring her to La Coruña for repairs . . .

"I'm sorry, Benito. I would have told you so sooner, but that would have meant revealing our plan. Which, by the way, you almost succeeded in foiling completely."

"I, señor? How can that be? Until this moment I didn't know a plan existed."

"You nearly destroyed it just the same. You see, once the boat was remodeled, Ramón and Pepe were to fish from Amor Milagroso. But after attacking two highly respected fishermen . . ."

Benito chuckled. "Paco and I drove them out of town."

"I see nothing humorous in that."

"Forgive me, señor. I was just thinking how amazing it is that two simple men—"

"Nowadays two simple men could blow up the world. That's not the point. The point is, besides being forced to live somewhere else, Ramón sprained his back and can hardly walk, much less embark on a mission. Which means unless I find another man who knows the sea, knows this part of the coast, and, above all, believes as we do . . ."

Benito swallowed dryly. "Your grace is suggesting that on the night of the *Romería,* I be waiting on that boat with Pepe."

The duke leaned back and smiled. "Not only will you save

the life of one of the greatest humanitarians Spain has ever known, you'll serve in the process an even higher cause."

"A higher cause, your grace?"

"Freedom. Truth. Call it what you will."

"Ah, yes."

"Of course, you'll also have sold your statues."

"I see. That, then, is the nature of our partnership. I help Pepe on the boat; your grace buys the golden figures."

"Well, not exactly. But you can be sure the buyer I choose will be sympathetic to our ideals."

"Our ideals. Sí, señor."

"Naturally, you'll receive the lion's share of the profits."

"Naturally . . ."

"Perhaps you'd like a moment to think."

A moment? Was that all it took to decide whether or not to risk one's life for a higher cause? Yet that wasn't the real issue: life against death. Death came to everyone. It wasn't even a case of whether he preferred to die at the *Romería* or some unknown moment in the future. That couldn't be decided in advance because for all he knew he could be killed going home from the villa. No, the issue was whether or not he was willing to risk his life for Don Diego . . . or, no, for Octavio Mora . . . or, no, for the cause Octavio Mora believed in. Which, in essence, was the cause Federico Bazán had believed in. *Por Dios,* was it then a question of how loyal he was to the memory of his father?

"I was just thinking," the duke said softly. "Once Mora is safely out of the firth, what need will I have for a boat like *La Mariposa*? Tell me, Benito, could an item like that adequately repay a man for risking his life?"

"It might, señor. Yet how could he explain how such a magnificent gift came into his possession?"

"He could say he bought it from the duke of Última Alegría, who, in gratitude for having been allowed to purchase the statues, agreed to persuade the previous owners to sell it and return to Vigo."

"Then the boat would become mine the night of the *Romería*."

"Exactly. And the trip up the firth your way of celebrating."

"Then it would seem the *Romería* would be the time your grace received the statues."

"Of course the funds might not be available on that date."

"But I'd have the boat, señor. Should I survive my celebration, I could go back to being a fisherman."

"But not for long. You'll be a rich and honored man, Benito, remember that."

"*Sí,* señor. But just in case . . . the boat would go to my son Manolo?"

"You have my word."

Benito smiled and lifted his glass. "Then by all means, your grace, let's drink to a long life for Octavio Mora."

# PART IV 🌿🌸🌿

# chapter 24

Shortly before noon on the twenty-fifth of July, Pablo Estrada stood in the library next to his office, appraising his appearance in a full-length mirror.

Yes, his thirteenth-century costume still fit him well: the blue velvet tunic set off his broad shoulders and narrow waist; the ermine collar, those intriguing streaks of white in his abundant black hair. The white leggings were good, too. Showed to advantage his straight, muscular legs. One would never take him for a man well over sixty.

He sighed, remembering the young widow, Señora Van der Linden, sitting beside him at Mass. How beautiful she had looked as the sun, streaming through the stained-glass windows, spangled her hair with jewels of colored light. Ay, it had made his heart ache just to look at her. And then to have to leave Mass early. He hoped she and everyone else realized it wasn't a lack of religious zeal that had made him sneak away, but rather, the press of his civic duties. After all, if the mayor wasn't waiting on the balcony when his distinguished guests stepped out of their limousines, how could he welcome them to the *Romería*?

Tightening his wide velvet belt, Pablo Estrada strode to the window and looked down on the brightly dressed crowd, milling around the central plaza. Ay, so many people. Except for the annual feast day in Santiago de Compostela, this must be Galicia's most popular festival. There were revelers everywhere. On roofs, on balconies, at windows, in the streets, huddled in doorways. And somewhere in that noisy, jostling throng were two agents from the *Dirección General de Promoción del Turismo*. What was their decision? That the mayor was right and Amor Milagroso was worthy of being declared a village of historic and artistic importance? By heaven, on a day like this what else could they think? Never had the sky seemed so blue, the air so fresh, the sun so invigorating. Truly, on a day like this a man could consider living in Amor Milagroso forever. Especially with a woman like Gabrielle Van der Linden beside him. But that couldn't be. The señora was American, which meant in less than a week she'd be flying across the sea, out of his life.

Turning from the window, the mayor pulled back his velvet cuff and consulted his watch. Five after twelve. Father Juan was running late, and the crowd would soon become restless. Start setting off firecrackers. Maybe even send up a few skyrockets. Still, that would be the first sign of anarchy either the men from *Turismo* or Octavio Mora would have witnessed. Until now the people of Amor Milagroso had been as docile as any bureaucrat from Madrid could deem possible.

Yes, so far everything about Mora's visit had been perfect. The weather. The dinner last night at Don Diego's. Though to anyone who knew him it was clear the duke had been preoccupied. But who could blame him? The poor man hadn't heard from his son or Erik Frostmann or Gabrielle's aunt in what?—eight, ten days now? Just as in all that time the mayor hadn't heard who was responsible for ransacking Benito Bazán's farm. Which meant things weren't as tranquil as they appeared on the surface. So it was good the mayor had stationed extra guards along the highway and borrowed that gunboat from his friend up in La Coruña.

Suddenly from the far side of the plaza came the joyous peal of church bells. That was his cue. Smiling broadly, the mayor stepped out onto the balcony and approached the railing, taking care not to stand too close, considering the tragic fate of his uncle Gregorio.

Pushed from behind by a young priest, Father Juan popped from the car like an enormous ripe olive. Then, balance regained, he set off across the plaza, blessing young and old, rich and poor, citizen and stranger.

Quite a crowd this year. But why hadn't more of them come to church? Pagan, that was what these *Romerías* were. Pagan. In spite of the Mass, the medals, the heavy gold cross they carried all the way to the *Romería* grounds. Which weren't even on the site of the supposed miracle. Oh, no, because that would mean the pilgrims would have to climb a couple of hills. Which would be a lot harder pilgrimage than merely strolling along the cliffs to the meadow next to the Villa Alegre. Bah. These villagers weren't thanking God for the blessing that had been bestowed on Don Luis; they were praying the same blessing would be bestowed on them. Which was why they insisted Benito's statues be included in the procession. Blasphemy, that was what that was. Blasphemy.

"Thank you, my child. Peace be with you," he murmured

as a blushing young woman slipped a wreath of red carnations around his neck, then kissed him demurely on his apple cheek. Ah, these bedazzled virgins with love gleaming in their eyes. Next spring there'd be the usual rash of baptisms. With or without a series of hasty weddings in the fall.

Saddened by his musings on human frailty, the priest raised his eyes to the balcony and the mayor. Ridiculous old popinjay. If Pablo only knew how those leggings emphasized his skinny old legs.

Shaking his head, Father Juan started up the stairs, aware the heat and the crowds were making him cranky. Aware, too, that he'd have to hide his mood in deference to the air of celebration. Perhaps when he reached the meadow he'd have a soothing glass of wine. And later, as a special treat, a platter or two of fried octopus.

Watching the mayor greet the priest, José arched his back and flexed his shoulders. It was tiring, standing so long in his thin-soled patent leather shoes. He'd be glad when the statues were delivered and he and María could slip away to enjoy the celebration.

Ah, María, with those rustling petticoats and tight white stockings. That hair hanging down her back. And those eyes. That smile. A month ago he wouldn't have believed he could feel this way about anyone. Especially a girl from the country. But now, even if the statues were never sold, even if he had to work in Madrid forever, he knew he couldn't go on living without being married to María del Carmen.

He swallowed, aware tomorrow was the day he must climb on the bus and start back to the city. Besides being apart from María, how was he going to endure the crowds, the noise, the yellow-brown air reeking of diesel fumes? Not that

Amor Milagroso was perfect. Far from it. But today . . . the air, the sun, the flags, the flowers. Ay, how fantastic the village of his birth! And more fantastic yet, the woman at his side . . . demure and lovely María del Carmen.

Head bowed, Concepción tried to keep her mind on Father Juan's prayer, but instead kept hearing and feeling the people around her. At last she abandoned the effort. Raised her head and opened her eyes.

How handsome everyone looked today, the women in their full skirts and embroidered aprons, the men in jackets, cummerbunds, and knee-length black pants. They looked like wealthy landowners, every one of them, even if their festival clothes had been handed down from generation to generation. Concepción was lucky she hadn't had to adjust her waistband since the birth of her daughter—might she rest in peace—fifteen years before. Weight wasn't a problem for Peralta women, though it obviously was for others, judging from the triangular inserts she spied in neighboring skirts as a mischievous breeze occasionally flipped up a shawl. And could it be that as a result of seeing the statues a lot more waistbands were going to receive even larger inserts over the next few months? If so, would any of the women in Amor Milagroso do what those women were doing in Italy? Impossible. Yet how would she—Concepción Elena Peralta de Bazán—feel if at age fifty she again found herself with child? Certainly she had given her body ample opportunity.

Again she bowed her head and tried to follow what the priest was saying. Yet with her eyes open, all that came to her mind was that her flat black slippers desperately needed polishing. Strange that with all the preparing of clothes she'd done last night, she'd forgotten even to brush them. But oh, didn't her menfolk look nice? She glanced sideways at José, whose white shirt was immaculate and whose city suit was neatly mended and carefully pressed—thanks to the weight of the double mattress. Then at Manolo, whose fisherman's shoulders threatened the seams of José's old bolero. Then at Benito. Poor Benito. How tired and anxious he looked, though his festival clothes said here is a man prepared to enjoy himself.

Concepción sighed, and raising her eyes to the balcony, discovered that not only had Father Juan finished his prayer but Pablo Estrada had completed his words of welcome and was even now signaling the band. Within seconds a vague approximation of a sprightly tune called *"Amor Milagroso, Milagro de Amor"* resounded in the warm midday air.

Concepción drew in her breath. She loved that song. It made her feel part of something. Proud of it. Aware that no matter its faults, that something—her village—had pre-vailed for centuries and was likely to prevail forever. Despite the mayor, the priest, the duke, or even the soldiers and police milling around the edge of the plaza.

The song ended, and tears welled in her eyes. Impatiently she brushed them away so she could see the tall, white-haired man standing at the flag-draped railing. By heaven, what right did an arrogant Castilian have to talk about Don Luis and the miracle? Mora didn't care about this village. He'd come here—no doubt at government expense—to visit his friend the duke, eat rich food, ride fine horses, and do whatever else people did in that gloomy pile of rocks west of the village. Bah! Such hypocrisy made her sick. Yet how shameful to think such uncharitable thoughts on a day honoring the rebirth of love and the founding of a village. She should feel grateful Mora and his family journeyed all this way just to speak at today's celebration. And she had to admit the man had a noble bearing as he stood, straight and tall, speaking to them of love and the power it had to remake the world.

Yes, she should really be more charitable, she decided, and bowing her head, breathed a silent prayer for Mora, his family, and, God willing, the statues' safe arrival into the hands of Don Diego.

The crowd cheered and whistled, some firecrackers went off, and six dozen balloons were released by the owner of a shoe store.

Benito grunted, dropped his cigarette, and crushed it to a pulp beneath the heel of his shoe.

He wasn't sure what he'd expected Mora to say, but certainly more than what a nice village this was and how happy he was to be here. Something that might justify a man's risking his life so the speaker would have a chance to speak elsewhere.

"You look worried," Concepción said. "Is everything all right?"

"Fine, fine," he muttered, and for perhaps the thirtieth time that day, inspected the ropes that bound the newly carved chest to the oxcart. *Bien.* All was secure. The treasure could neither slip from its bed of flowers nor be pulled from the cart without someone's having a sharp knife and the willingness to kill Benito, his sons, and the four guards sent by Don Diego.

Relieved, he straightened up and surveyed the crowd. Never had he seen so many people in Amor Milagroso. And in each of the streets radiating from the plaza a group of eight or ten soldiers, plus four or five members of the *Guardia Civil.* He couldn't remember seeing such an obvious display of governmental force at a local celebration. But whether the troops had been called out because the mayor wanted to maintain the peace in front of Octavio Mora, or because the mayor had had word Mora himself was a threat to peace, there was no way of knowing.

Benito swallowed and rubbed his hand over his newly shaved chin, thinking, with all these guards tonight's expedition might be more dangerous than he'd imagined. As for transporting the statues to the meadow . . . so far as he could tell, Don Miguel wasn't around, nor was his friend Señor Frostmann. But the smugglers—who could say? They could be anywhere and everywhere, despite the soldiers, the *Guardia,* and that gunboat Manolo had seen in a secluded cove west of the villa . . .

A round of applause brought Benito's attention back to the plaza. Near the fountain that marked the beginning of the parade, *el gran gaitero* himself, Eliseo Rabal, had pumped up his bagpipes, and the strains of a sprightly march written by his cousin Joaquín were wheezing from *pianissimo* to *forte.* A few seconds later Eliseo signaled the crowd, and accompanied by one son on flute and another on drum, set off for one of the narrow, winding streets that led to the coastal highway. Next went Alfonso Lozano, the doctor, César Soto, the dentist, and Claudio Díaz, the pharmacist, carrying, respectively, the flags of Spain, Galicia, and Amor Milagroso. Behind them, with an air of solemnity, walked Roberto López and Manuel Piedra, sharing the weight of an eighteen-meter pole topped by a crucifix. Behind them, slightly out of step, marched the mayor, the priest, and the duke of Última Alegría.

"Now you, Benito," a man called out.

"No, *hombre,*" he shouted back. "I don't want to follow the priest. I want to follow the dancing girls."

The crowd laughed and waved, and as if on cue a troupe of costumed dancers ran forward and fell in line, skipping and twirling. Then, before Benito could goad the oxen, six villagers, each wearing an enormous papier-mâché head, ran out from under a balcony. As usual, one of the heads represented Don Luis, one his bride, Doña Anita, one a turbaned Moor, and one a leering red devil. The last two, however, were new—a laughing man and a laughing woman, each painted a shimmering gold.

"The lovers!" someone shouted, and the crowd went wild. Fearful of panic, Benito prodded his beribboned beasts, and followed by a host of high-spirited villagers, set off on his pilgrimage.

As the *Romería* procession wound through the streets, in the woods that bordered the meadow a perspiring Don Miguel fanned his darkened face with a leaf from a plane tree. My, it was getting warm. And it would be even worse later on. He shuddered, glad this year at least he wouldn't have to stroll through the foul-smelling mob, playing lord of the manor. Still, it would seem odd, viewing the festivities from the bushes. And when he did venture forth, keeping his head bowed, his eyes averted. Because he didn't trust this ridiculous disguise. He'd told Erik not to go to a costume shop, but oh, no. That soft Danish skin could be encased only in something silky and pretty. Above all, sanitary. Those Nordics. They were enough to drive a hot-blooded Latin insane. Imagine, not having the slightest idea a nobleman might feel upset, costumed like a third-rate comedian. Or skulking in the bushes with a gaggle of hired hoodlums. Or, worst of all, planning to steal from one's very own father . . .

At the edge of the village the dancers and "big heads" scrambled onto the bed of an ancient truck; the civic triumvirate eased their privileged bodies into a waiting Mercedes; the old, the sick, and the weary climbed into assorted conveyances or onto the backs of various animals; and the few pilgrims who'd elected to walk struck off on the grassy path that followed the ins and outs of the coastal bluffs all the way to the villa.

Benito breathed deeply of the tangy salt air, then gazed down at the sea and the shoreline. By heaven, it was beautiful here. And this procession . . . with all his worries he'd forgotten how enjoyable it really was, the women gossiping to their heart's content, the men passing around the goatskin wine flasks. Smiling, he reached for Concepción's hand.

"In truth, it's a glorious day," he observed.

"Perhaps too glorious. Already six couples have abandoned the procession for the woodland."

"And what's wrong with that?"

"Benito, have you no shame?"

"Not today, *mujer*. Today, were it not for my responsibility, I would run into that woodland myself. Provided you agreed to come with me."

"Devil." She laughed, and Benito grinned, thinking how wonderful it would be if love were always the force that made people do things. Not just the love of a man for a woman, but the love he suddenly felt for everybody. Indeed, for everything. The grass, the trees, the sunlight, the water. Then it hit him. Considering what he'd be doing that night, this might well be his last day on earth.

Heart pounding, he dropped his wife's hand, pretending an urgent need to wipe his brow with his shirt sleeve. Incredible to think that tomorrow at this time this coast and these people would still exist, while he . . .

"No," he murmured, "no."

"Benito, what's wrong?" Concepción asked, eyes anxious.

"Nothing, nothing."

"With a face like that?"

"The sun . . . Get me the wine flask."

"I'll be back in a minute. José has it."

Benito nodded absently and turned to the oxcart, creaking along beside him. On that bed of flowers, inside that miniature casket, the golden lovers lay wrapped like mummies for their trip to the villa. And after that, where would they go? Some foreign mansion? A museum? A bank vault? Who could tell, but as far as Benito was concerned, this procession was their funeral.

Overcome with sadness—for himself as well as his treasure—he raised his eyes to the distant hillside. There was where the lovers should be put to rest. Where they'd lain for centuries, in the cave beneath the oak grove. Yes, that would be proper, for the statues might well be what had cured Don Luis. Which meant they were the very lifeblood of the village.

But if that were true . . . ay, if that were true . . . what right did Benito have to sell them to anyone?

# chapter 25

What with the slow pace of the oxen and the pilgrims' frequent stops to share wine or void that which had accumulated, it was midafternoon before the procession finally arrived at the *Romería* grounds. By that time the band was already on the bandstand playing what passed in Amor Milagroso for rock 'n roll, while below them on the large wooden dance platform a few daring couples and about a dozen young girls tried to keep step with the, at best, unusual rhythms.

Tired, out of sorts, headachy from the wine, the sun, and his disturbing thoughts, Benito guided the oxen past the platform to the shade of a maple tree. There, ignoring the music and the gathering crowd as best he could, he again checked the ropes; then, wiping his brow, told his sons to take care of the beasts while he and Concepción got something to eat at the *Romería* house.

"Do you think that's wise?" Concepción asked, laying a restraining hand on her husband's shirt sleeve. "In truth, I would feel happier remaining with the treasure until—"

"Ah, Benito, there you are," called Eliseo Rabal, elbowing his way through the onlookers. "Listen, I've just had a wonderful idea. When you give the duke the statues, my sons and I will sanctify the event with music."

Benito groaned. "As far as I'm concerned, the less ceremony the better."

"Then why deliver them in public at all?" Eliseo snapped, obviously annoyed by the rejection.

"So the duke can make a speech," Benito told him.

"Ha. About what?"

"How do I know about what? Am I in the man's confidence? I suppose so everyone will know he's receiving the figures with my blessing."

"And is he?"

"You think I'd fulfill my bargain with a curse?"

"Right now I'd say—"

"Look, *papá*! There he comes!" Manolo cried, pointing to

the black-suited nobleman approaching the dance floor in the company of Pablo Estrada, Father Juan, and the family of Octavio Mora.

"Excuse me," sniffed Eliseo, "but if I can't pipe the main event, at least I'm going to pipe the preliminaries." And off he went, beckoning to his sons to join him.

"You know what I think?" asked Paco Camino, who, having ridden to the meadow on a truck, now leaned, relaxed and refreshed, against the trunk of the maple tree. "I think you're beginning to have second thoughts. That you don't really want to deliver those statues at all."

"Quiet, old man," Benito muttered. "What do you know?"

"I know that I, too, will be sorry to see the treasure go, Benito. As will the craftsmen. And Teresa León. And—"

"What do I care about Teresa León?" barked Benito. "Or the craftsmen? Not to mention every male in this accursed village."

"Amor Milagroso isn't cursed, Benito, it's blessed. That's what we're celebrating. The day Don Luis received the blessing."

"Ay, what have I done to be surrounded by fools! One more word about blessings and . . . ay, how can anyone think with Eliseo's pipes producing that god-awful wailing?"

"Benito, what's wrong?" Concepción asked. "You're acting like a man possessed."

"He is," Paco chuckled. "By the thought of giving up those golden figures."

"Leave me in peace!" Benito shouted. "I'm going for some wine, and if no one wants to go with me—"

Concepción grabbed his arm. "Listen, *hombre*. The pipes have stopped."

"Hallelujah!" Benito cried, and turned to his sons. "Now remember, José, don't untie those ropes until I give you the signal."

"Citizens and friends . . ." said Pablo Estrada from the dance floor, and after adjusting the microphone, welcomed everyone to the meadow, gave those who might not know a brief history of the statues, then said that the duke of Última Alegría would now receive this magnificent treasure from the hands of the humble fisherman who found it.

The crowd whistled and clapped, and a boy in short trousers ran to the bandstand and beat on the big bass drum. The mayor waved him away, then looked anxiously over the audience.

"If Benito Bazán would now come forward . . ."

"Bah. He doesn't give a man time to think," Benito muttered.

"What's there to think about?" Concepción asked. "There's the platform. There's the duke. All you have to do is—"

"I know, I know. Am I a simpleton?"

"Lately I don't know what you are."

"Perhaps he's nervous," Manolo suggested.

"Me?" Benito cried, "a man who spoke to a hundred people in a café? Greeted pilgrims from all parts of the province?"

And, straightening his cummerbund, strode out from under the tree. Humble fisherman, indeed. Pablo Estrada didn't know what he was talking about. Yet why did the mayor's words make him angry, Benito wondered as, waving to his friends, he stepped up onto the dance floor. If he survived this night, wasn't that what he wanted to be? A humble fisherman . . .

"At last," the mayor muttered as he greeted Benito with a bland smile and an indifferent handshake. Then, with a sweep of his velvet-clad arm, directed the crowd's attention to the duke. Don Diego acknowledged their cheers with an aristocratic nod, then walked briskly to the microphone and in a sharp, clear voice told them how happy he was to have been given the task of finding a permanent home for such a significant masterpiece. In fact, so grateful did he feel that before receiving the statues, he wished to announce he'd be making a generous contribution to each of the village charities.

"And in gratitude to the man who made this all possible," the duke went on, "I've caused to have delivered to my dock a certain well-known fishing boat."

Benito started. What? *La Mariposa* at the duke's private dock? That must mean the plans had been changed.

"Don't just stand there," the mayor rasped. "Give him the statues."

Feeling a bit dazed, Benito looked out across the sea of faces. Focused at last on José and gave him the signal. Faithful to his instructions, the young man untied the ropes, then moved out of the way as one of Don Diego's guards picked up the chest, and the other three, guns drawn, escorted him through the crowd.

Benito watched them approach, struck by how different this was from the day he'd scurried down the hill, cradling the original box like a baby. Poor little statues. Never again would they watch a middle-aged couple make love on a cold stone floor. Or see farmers and fishermen file solemnly past, their faces reflecting both shame and anticipation. What a pity it all had to end. The lovers go wherever Fate might take them. He and Concepción back to what they were doing before. And the farmers and fishermen? Without the farm as a place of pilgrimage, where could they gather to enjoy such an uplifting experience?

"No," he murmured, accepting the box and hugging it to his chest.

"What did you say?" asked Pablo Estrada.

"No!"

"No, what?"

Benito shook his head. "I've changed my mind. I can't go through with it."

The mayor's face went livid. "What do you mean, you can't go through with it?"

Benito shook his head again.

Hand over the microphone, the mayor turned to the duke. "He says he can't go through with it."

"I know. I heard," said Don Diego.

"What's happening? What's wrong?" voices called from the audience.

"One moment . . . it seems we have a problem." Leaving the microphone, the mayor stalked to where Benito stood as though spellbound. "What are you doing?" he demanded. "Don't you know Octavio Mora is watching every—" He stopped, fought to control his anger. "All right," he said. "Don't just stand here like a clod. If you're going back on your word, go over to the duke and tell him."

Benito nodded, and tucking the chest under his arm, started toward the small, white-haired man regarding him with a puzzled expression. Going back on his word—was that what Benito was doing? *Por Dios,* what was he going to say? What was he going to do next?

"Benito, what's happened?" asked Don Diego, leading him from both the mayor and the microphone.

"I don't know, señor. But I'm sorry. I can't go through with it."

The duke's face became glacial. "If you recall, you and I had an agreement."

Benito glanced at Octavio Mora, his wife, and two sons, who were sitting on folding chairs next to the bandstand. "Your grace has no need to become alarmed," he said softly. "I'm not saying I've changed my mind about—"

"Quiet! The very air could be our enemy."

Benito lowered his voice. "I give you my word, señor. That part of our agreement which concerns someone else shall not be violated."

"And what is causing you to violate the rest?"

"I'm not sure, señor. Maybe what we were talking about up at the villa."

The duke frowned. "And what was that?"

"Loyalty to a higher cause, your grace."

"Ah, yes. Which is?"

"All of us, señor. Not just me. Not just your grace and his cause. All of us."

"Strange words, Benito, coming from a man who professes to be a Spaniard."

"An Amor Milagrosan, your grace. Which is why I'm certain the statues have to remain here."

Pablo Estrada suddenly appeared at the duke's elbow. "Excuse me, Diego, but have you managed to comprehend what this imbecile is saying?"

Don Diego sighed. "It seems, my dear Pablo, our friend has suffered an acute attack of altruism."

"And what does that mean?"

"The statues stay here."

"If he intends turning that farm into a permanent—"

"Pablo, please . . ." The duke raised a weary hand. "Another minute and our more passionate observers are going to climb on this platform and hear for themselves what we're talking about."

"But you can't just . . . this man promised to—"

"If I can accept his change of heart, surely you can," the duke said softly.

"Peasants," muttered the mayor. "Call them what you will—fellow citizens, fellow countrymen—they're still peasants, and I say you can't trust them."

"Perhaps not," the duke agreed, "yet with all our advantages, I wonder . . . but that's beside the point, isn't it?" His smile faded as again he turned to Benito.

"You realize, of course, that by refusing to deliver the statues you've forfeited your chance of owning *La Mariposa*?"

Benito sagged as the full meaning of what he'd done finally struck him. "*Sí*, señor," he mumbled. "It hadn't occurred to me, but yes, it's only fair."

"I'm glad you agree," the duke said coldly. Then turned back to the scowling mayor. "I suggest, Pablo, that you inform our fellow citizens of the change in plans. Then give them something amusing to look at so we won't be confronted with pandemonium."

"But the statues," the mayor protested. "What's going to happen to the statues?"

"That's Benito's problem, not mine," said the duke, and beckoning to his guards, turned on his heel and started across the platform to Octavio Mora.

Clutching the wooden box, Benito stood as though rooted to the platform. What should he do? Run after the duke and tell him he'd changed his mind? Surely that would be the most reasonable thing to do. If nothing else, to find out where and when he was supposed to rendezvous with Pepe. Though the duke, by refusing Benito the boat, had taken away Benito's excuse for either boarding her or being on the dock. Did Don Diego know that, he wondered; then, hearing shouts and whistles, realized Pablo Estrada had explained the change in plans and was now "calling upon our wonderful traveling players to present that most delightful of plays, 'The Miracle of Amor Milagroso.'"

There was a round of applause, then, as the costumed actors and actresses pushed toward the platform, Eliseo's son pounded his drum.

"Another miracle!" he shouted. "The statues are ours. *Vivan los célticos!*"

The crowd came to life.

"*Vivan los célticos!*"

"*Vivan los célticos!*"

"*Vivan los célticos!*"

"Go back, go back," the mayor implored as a dozen men leaped to the platform, and before Benito could do a thing, raised him to the shoulders of Andrés Rabal and Ignacio León.

Fighting for balance, Benito tucked the chest in his armpit and with his free hand clutched at Ignacio's hair.

"*Viva* Benito!"

"*Viva* Benito!"

"*Viva* Benito!" chanted the crowd.

"Put me down, put me down," Benito hollered.

"Here, give the statues to me," called Roberto López.

"No! No!" Benito yelled. "Nobody gets to— Aaayyyy!!!" Teetering precariously as his bearers jumped from the platform and started running through the crowd. Suddenly he lurched to the side, and the box fell into the outstretched hands of Manuel Piedra.

"Take it to my sons!" Benito shouted.

"*Viva* Benito, *viva* Benito," the crowd kept chanting as its members clutched at his calves and slapped him on the rump.

"Ay, to think the statues will be in our village forever," a woman crooned, tears streaming down her face.

"I'll be up there tomorrow," a man called out.

"My cousin will come here from Orense!"

"My family will make the journey from León!"

"No, no," Benito shouted, looking wildly around the meadow. "Manolo! José! Help me!"

"Ay, Benito, what have you done?" shrieked Concepción, pushing through the howling mob.

"Nothing, *mujer,* nothing."

"Nothing! You told him you wouldn't sell. Why?"

"It had to be," he bellowed. "The people demanded it."

"And who are you? Their king?"

Firecrackers crackled an answer, and at the edge of the meadow a skyrocket sizzled into the sky.

"*Amigos,* for the love of heaven, put me down!" Benito shouted.

"Not here," gasped Ignacio. "They'd tear bits from your clothing for holy relics."

"Then take me into the woods."

"In truth, I can't carry him much longer," Andrés confessed.

"Air, air, give him air," shouted Ignacio, and as the crowd fell back, the two men—half running, half staggering—carried their burden into the woods. Meanwhile, up on the platform, the music swelled, signaling the start of the performance. The crowd, torn between following the village hero or feasting their eyes on a once-a-year production, opted for the latter and drifted en masse back to the dance floor.

"You've done a fine thing this day," Ignacio panted as he and his partner set Benito down under a plane tree.

"Truly inspiring," agreed Andrés, wiping his brow.

"To think Amor Milagroso will have a shrine of its own," Ignacio went on, "as famous in its way as Covadonga or the caves I have heard spoken of in Altamira."

"We never wanted that Granflaqueza to sell those statues," Andrés reported, "but we didn't dare speak out, knowing after what happened that day on the farm, you couldn't protect the lovers forever."

"You're right. I couldn't. I can't," Benito panted. "I've got to get back. Now that the duke's guards aren't— Wait! What was that?"

"It sounded like gunfire," cried Andrés.

Panicky, Benito ran toward the meadow, aware of men shouting, women screaming, horses whinnying. Then a motor roared and gunfire sounded again.

Gasping for breath, he ran out from under the trees. Saw men on horseback, galloping toward the highway. A Jeep, already on the road, racing toward the village. Police and soldiers scrambling into trucks. And around the oxcart, people moaning, weeping, wiping their eyes.

"What is it? What happened?" he demanded.

"Tear gas," a man shouted.

"Ay, Benito, they got it, they got it," wailed Paco.

"Who?" Benito persisted. "Who did this thing?"

"Men with guns and horses. At least a dozen, Benito. They came charging out of the woodland."

"But who were they?"

"Smugglers," Concepción answered, blowing her nose.

"And in the Jeep?" Benito asked.

"God knows," José replied. "They all wore gas masks."

"And I thought I saw some Gypsies," Manolo added.

"Ay, Benito, what are we going to do?" moaned Paco.

"See if there are any horses left in the corral."

"No, Benito, no," Concepción cried, pulling at her husband's arm. "With all those police, the thieves will be caught before they're halfway to the village."

"Maybe so, but I'm still going after them," Benito insisted, and shaking free of his wife's grasp, ran toward the woodland.

"Wait," shouted Paco. "I'm going with you."

"No!" Concepción called after them. "Benito, come back. It's hopeless. They have a head start."

"They may have a head start," he hollered over his shoulder, "but if it's El Chavo and his men, I alone know where they're going."

# chapter 26

"You may know where you're going," grumbled Paco Camino as his burro scrambled to keep its footing on the steep incline, "but in truth I'd feel more at ease if someone else had left the highway with us."

"They probably thought we were taking a shortcut to the farm," Benito called from his horse. "You have to agree, it was clever of El Chavo to send the Jeep to the village while he took my treasure directly to the cave."

"If, in fact, that was what he did."

"What else would he do, *amigo*?"

"Am I an expert in the ways of smugglers?" Paco demanded. "It's all I can do to follow the rump of your horse up this accursed mountain."

"Someday, my friend, you're going to have to get new glasses. I can see as though it were noon. Look. Up there's the ridge. Then we round those boulders, cross a stream, and end up in the oak grove."

"And if we don't stop, we can go down the opposite slope and end up safe in our beds. But ay, Benito, think! Who wants to be in bed on the night of the *Romería*?"

"Quiet! You'll attract their attention."

"I thought you said they were riding toward the village."

"But they must have sentinels. Use your head, old man."

"This is crazy, Benito. We have no guns. Not even a club. What are we doing here?"

"Go back if you're so afraid."

"I can't go back," Paco howled. "I can't see my way down the trail. Ay, if only I'd taken that train to Milan."

"Shhhhh. What was that?"

"I didn't hear anything."

"There. Behind those trees. Isn't that a—"

"Well, well, if it isn't Don Quixote and Sancho Panza," thundered a voice. "Only this time the fat one's on the horse, and the crazy one's on the burro."

"What shall we do, Benito? Run for it?"

Benito shook his head. "We're doomed, *viejo*. They'd blow our heads off before we were halfway down the hill."

# chapter 27 🦋🌸🦋

At dusk the generators began to throb and strands of yellow lights formed a glowing golden "X" above the dance floor. Gradually, as though the artificial suns invited improvisation, the band started experimenting and dancers who all afternoon had been self-conscious and stiff now whirled and dipped with unconscious abandon. But while the dancers grew ever more free and the rhythms more bold, Concepción, indifferent to the lights, the music, the crowds, stood beside the empty oxcart telling herself that the police, the soldiers, the *Guardia Civil* were doing all that was humanly possible. That in the meantime it was only natural the *Romería* continue. Only natural that people dance and drink as though nothing out of the ordinary had happened. As though tomorrow morning life would proceed as usual. Well, maybe for them it would. But for Concepción Peralta de Bazán, unless her menfolk came back, life in many respects would be over.

She shivered, and drawing her shawl closer around her shoulders, decided she'd be better off walking around, asking for news, seeing if by some chance Benito and her sons had come back to the meadow and were even now entering the *Romería* house. Warmed by this hope, she asked María del Carmen to stay with the cart, told her to come after

Concepción the minute there was any word, then eased into the milling, boisterous crowd, eager for news but finding only broad backs, fat stomachs, sharp elbows. So on she went, reeling from the smells—garlic, sweat, tobacco, alcohol—flinching at the drunken laughs, the groping hands, the ribald requests. At last, gasping for breath, she arrived at the open space in front of the food booths. Here trestle tables had been set up and were now surrounded by laughing families, eating and drinking. How happy these people were, she thought, and how indifferent to the plight of others. Even the man who only hours before they'd acclaimed as the village hero.

She blinked away some self-pitying tears, and when her eyes cleared, set off for the small, unpainted house where every year pilgrims went to buy wine, beer, cold meats, and bread, and, most important, to sit on the long wooden benches, smoking, laughing, exchanging ideas and information. Then, as she was nearing the door, someone called out to her.

She whirled. Saw Pablo Estrada beckoning from a table under a pine tree.

"Any news?" the mayor asked, as if she were directing the search rather than he.

"No, señor," she said, drawing closer. "That's why I'm going to the *Romería* house."

The mayor grunted, and she noticed his face was flushed with wine, as was the face of Señora Van der Linden, and, as usual, the face of Father Juan. However, the rest of the group—Señor Mora, his wife, his two grown sons, Don Diego—seemed ill at ease, even anxious. Could it be possible they were worried about Benito, too?

"Well, if you don't hear anything, don't be upset," Pablo

Estrada advised her. "The thieves will be found. You have my word for it."

"*Sí,* señor. Thank you."

"We have the army, the *Guardia,* and we can't forget our own excellent police force. Which reminds me, Diego," he said, turning to the duke. "About an hour ago, my men found some unknown ruffian loitering on your dock."

The duke stiffened. "A man on my— What did they do with him?"

"What do you suppose? Took him to jail."

"My God."

"What's wrong? Surely you don't feel sorry for the bastard."

"That depends," the duke said coldly. "You see, that might have been the man I hired to bring *La Mariposa* from Las Palomillas. And take her back again. If it is, you've subjected him, and me, to a great deal of inconvenience."

"According to my men, he didn't have a scrap of identification," the mayor muttered. "What were they to do?"

"Nothing. Because they shouldn't have been there in the first place. For centuries the Villa Alegre has stood on that cliff, inviolate."

Concepción coughed. "If your grace will excuse me . . ."

"Yes, yes. I forgot you were even here," the mayor mumbled. "But as I said before, don't worry. We have the army, the *Guardia,* the police . . . and if they try to escape by boat . . ." He chuckled. "They'll find Pablo Estrada has a little surprise for them."

Octavio Mora raised shaggy white eyebrows. "A surprise? What would that be?"

"Not that I was expecting any trouble," the mayor said

quickly, "but these days one never knows . . . Revolutionaries. Terrorists. Disgraceful . . ."

"But what's your surprise?" Father Juan asked with a burp.

The mayor beamed. "One of the fastest gunboats in Galicia. And six men prepared to stop any suspicious vessel." He laughed. "I only hope they don't shoot first and ask questions afterward."

"Oh, no," gasped Mora's wife, hand at her throat.

"Ah, señora, forgive me. Such talk on the evening of the *Romería* . . ." He shook his head, reached for the nearest bottle of wine. "Please, everyone. Drink! Enjoy yourselves!"

Benito shifted his shoulders, trying to find a position where the ropes wouldn't cut so deeply into his arms. Meanwhile El Chavo, all in black, breathed out another cloud of cigar smoke.

"So you think they'll be caught," the smuggler said. "Well, I think they'll take cover as planned and be back here within the hour. Then, *bueno,* see for yourself." Gesturing toward the stacks of cardboard boxes that lined the walls of the vaulted chamber. "We can stay here for days. Weeks if we have to."

Benito coughed. "If we don't all die from the foul-smelling air."

"Believe me, when you and your friend depart this life, it won't be the foul-smelling air that sends you."

"I don't see why we have to depart this life at all," Paco whined, shifting his buttocks on the rocky ledge. "We haven't done anything."

El Chavo smiled. "Let's say I feel obliged to keep up my men's morale. They don't like people stumbling into their hideaway."

"I thought you and I had an agreement," Benito muttered.

El Chavo raised his well-clipped eyebrows. "Us, Benito? You and me?"

"Don't play innocent, Vicente. You were supposed to come down to the farm and bargain with the man I thought was a buyer."

"Was I, indeed?"

"That was what you said."

"That was what you suggested. If you remember, you slid from your chair before we finished our conversation."

"I was sick."

"You were lucky. Had you been well, you might never have got home at all."

"Bah. You let me go because you hoped I'd lead you to the treasure."

"But you fooled me, didn't you? You surrounded it with innocent villagers."

"You could have attacked a thousand times, Vicente. Why didn't you?"

"What have we here? The prisoner interrogating his captor?"

"You could have killed my friends, slaughtered my family. But you didn't make a move. Why?"

"Let's say I had my reasons . . ."

"Then when you did attack, you couldn't find the safe. Benito Bazán had been too clever for you."

The smuggler crushed his cigar beneath the heel of his boot. "Benito Bazán is a fool . . . and always has been. I didn't attack your farm. Why should I? All I had to do was bide my time and get not only the statues but some wealthy coot worth a fortune in ransom."

"But I fooled you," Benito cried. "I wound up selling to

the local duke. Ay, the duke! Vicente, you've got to let me out of here."

"Never."

"You don't understand. It's not just me. There's someone I have to—"

"We all have someone, Benito," El Chavo sighed. "A wife, a mistress . . ."

"No. This is different. This is—"

"I hate dying men who whine."

"I'm not whining. There's a man out there who—" He glanced at the wide-eyed Paco. "Listen, Vicente, let me talk to you in private."

"Even in public your chatter's beginning to bore me."

"But the man may— Listen, you're against the same people I am. Let me at least tell you, so you can send someone else."

"And have them shot through the head by one of Pablo Estrada's idiots? Not on your life. Soriano!" he shouted. "Come over here and stand watch so I can have a moment's peace before Bruto gets back here with the raiders."

The moon was rising when Concepción, having completed her tour of the *Romería* house, and having avoided the crowd by circling around the rear of the bandstand, entered the woods, intending to make her quiet way back to the oxcart. Suddenly, in the shadows ahead, she saw a dozen men leading their horses to the corral. Eagerly she ran to the railing, only to learn the thieves had disappeared at the outskirts of the village. Taken refuge, no doubt, in some preplanned hideaway. And Benito? Not a sign. Though José and Manolo had been seen searching for him in the village.

Concepción thanked the men, and plodding toward the

cart, heard lively music punctuated by peals of joyous laughter. As she approached the meadow, she saw bonfires leaping into life. People singing, dancing, happy to be alive. And she? She didn't belong out there; she belonged here, where the birds were silent and the shadows comforting.

Turning abruptly, she started down a path that led to the bluff, remembering previous *Romerías* when she and Benito had slipped from the crowd to watch the sun sink slowly into the sea. Now, straining to follow the path in the dim moonlight, she stumbled over stones and brushed against branches until, reaching the cliff, she climbed to a familiar pile of rocks and breathed a silent prayer for the safe return of her beloved husband. Then, feeling a bit more calm, she raised her head and opened her eyes.

The air was soft, and at the base of the cliff the waves, as they broke, glowed with phosphorescent plankton. Ay, how beautiful was God's world . . . in the dark as well as in the sunlight. She smiled, and turning toward the duke's private cove, saw in the moonlight the dark outline of the dock and the darker mass she knew was *La Mariposa*.

Poor Benito, she thought, coming so close to owning that boat, then— No, she didn't even want to think about it. But she did have to think about the light that suddenly came on in the cabin. Who could that be, she wondered, and waited for the motor to throb, someone to cast off the lines, the boat to chug from the harbor. Nothing happened. Whoever had lighted that lamp seemed to be staying inside the cabin. A guard, perhaps. Because that man the police had arrested really was a ruffian and the duke was afraid there'd be others. But who in Amor Milagroso would want to steal or vandalize a fishing boat? Unless . . .

No, it couldn't be. Benito wasn't that crazy. Besides, he

and Paco had gone riding off after the thieves. Which didn't mean they couldn't have come back. That Benito, mourning the loss of his treasure, hadn't decided he'd at least get the boat.

But that would be insane. Benito wasn't a madman. Though she had to admit, in the past few days . . .

"No, Benito, no," she murmured. "Don't. It isn't worth it."

She moved to the edge of the cliff, gnawed at her lower lip. Chances were, whoever was down there, it wasn't Benito.

But if it was—dear God, if it was—and she did nothing to try to stop him . . .

Benito peered around the cave. In every large alcove five or six men were drinking wine and smoking cigarettes, while in a small room, barely visible under the stairs, El Chavo sat at a candlelit table on which were a bouquet of flowers and two wineglasses.

"Ay, Benito, what are we going to do?" moaned Paco.

Benito shook his head. Even if he could slip unnoticed from the ledge, crawl to the entrance of the tunnel, he wouldn't stand a chance. Not with his arms tied behind his back.

"Nothing," he muttered. "We sit here and wait."

"For what?"

"How should I know? Have I done this before?"

And with those words, realized he'd come full circle, back to the pagan altar. Only now, no shaft of sunlight lit up a shadowy niche, no ray of hope lightened his heavy heart. El Chavo was going to kill them. Or have them killed. What difference did it make? Either way, Benito and Paco were going to die. While Octavio Mora waited, and Concepción

. . . what was Concepción doing, he wondered. And his sons . . .

He swallowed dryly, strained again at his ropes. By heaven, the life wasn't out of him yet. He had to pull himself together. Think of a way to get out of this . . .

Holding up her skirt, Concepción jumped from the rocks and ran to where a steep trail snaked down to the beach. Then, slipping and sliding, down she went in the silvery moonlight.

Once on the sand, she sprinted to an outcropping of rock. Stopped. Knotted her shawl and kicked off her low black slippers. Then, shoes in one hand, crumpled-up skirt in the other, she waded forward. Mother of God, don't let me slip, she prayed, and rounding the rock, arrived chilled and panting in the duke's private cove.

For a moment she just stood there, catching her breath as she watched the light in *La Mariposa*'s cabin. Then, still holding her shoes and skirt, she scurried down the beach. Stopped at the dock, slipped her wet, sandy feet into her shoes, and tiptoed to the boat, which was moored sideways to the pier about a hundred meters from the shore.

Tense, ill at ease, she stared down at the nets, floats, lines, and poles that littered the tiny deck, then raised her eyes to the curtained window. What was she going to say if the person in the cabin was a guard? Or do if it was a thief, other than her Benito? She swallowed, aware of lapping waves, a gentle breeze, faint music behind her on the bluff.

Ay, what was she going to do? Board the boat, or turn on her heel and run silently back to the meadow?

She frowned. A coward? Concepción Peralta de Bazán? Never.

Stretching out a leg, she eased herself down onto the deck. How dark everything was, and how quiet. Holding her breath, she tiptoed through the clutter, raised her knuckles, and knocked on the cabin door.

Silence.

Then the click of a key, the creak of a hinge, and there stood a small, white-haired man dressed like a fisherman.

"Don Diego!" she gasped.

"And why not? Is this not my boat? My pier?"

"Assuredly, señor. I was just—"

She stopped, noticing a small gun aimed directly at her heart.

"What are you doing here, Señora Bazán?"

"I . . . I was looking for Benito."

"Aren't we all," sighed the duke, and lowered his weapon.

"Benito was supposed to take your grace fishing?" she suggested.

"What? No. Not exactly."

"But he was supposed to come here," she persisted.

The duke smiled. "Tell me, señora. Why would a man like me go fishing the night of the *Romería?*"

Who could say why a nobleman would do anything . . . "I don't know, señor," she answered.

"Then perhaps you know this. An experienced fisherman, could he handle a boat like this alone?"

"That would depend, señor."

"On what?"

"On the weather. How far he had to go. How good he was at telling direction from the stars."

The duke rubbed his chin. "It's been a long time . . . what? six, eight years since I sold the sloop? More than twelve since I got rid of the schooner."

Concepción nodded. "Your grace sold the sloop the summer José was relieved of his appendix. That would be eight years ago this coming August. And the schoooner sailed from this coast when Manolo was sick with the measles. Which would make it, as your grace said, twelve years ago last April."

"You have quite a memory, Señora Bazán."

"My sons mean a lot to me, señor."

"I mean about the boats. What makes you remember about my boats?"

She shrugged. "For twenty-five years, was I not the wife of a fisherman, señor?"

He studied her thoughtfully, then nodded. "Indeed you were, señora. Indeed you were. Tell me, what do you know about reading charts? Finding your way in a fog?"

"I señor? Nothing. But once when the fish were running and Benito's crew had the influenza, I learned to steer as good as any man. And raise a sail. And hold my own, pulling in the nets."

"Did you, indeed?"

"Sí, señor. As I just now told you."

"I'm sorry. I was thinking for a moment of . . . but no, that wouldn't be practical. On this trip we won't be concerned with pulling in nets, we'll be concerned with avoiding them."

He glanced at his watch. "Ah, it's getting late. I mustn't keep you. If you'd like a flashlight to—"

He stopped. Stared at the shore, where a dark figure jumped from the sand onto the dock.

"Someone's coming," he barked, and pushing Concepción to one side, stepped out on deck, drew his gun, and closed the cabin door.

•

"Mitsubishi! Mitsubishi!"

El Chavo ran out from under the stairs and stared up at the leafy trapdoor.

"Hitachi!" he bellowed.

The trapdoor creaked open, and down the steps came five dark-skinned men wearing flowered bandannas, pastel-colored satin shirts, and skin-tight black trousers.

"We caught them preparing an attack," shouted a grim-faced man who, from the top of the stairs, menaced the quintet with a revolver.

El Chavo laughed. "An attack? Them?"

"*Sí, mi jefe.* They had machine pistols and gas, but Julián and Pedro came down from the trees and took them by surprise."

"Good work," El Chavo said. Then, waving the sentry back to his post, surveyed the sullen group at the bottom of the stairs.

"So," he said, "you thought you could storm in here and get the treasure. All right. Who are you, how did you get here, and what are you doing in those ridiculous Gypsy costumes?"

Three of the newcomers—tall, burly men—shifted their shoulders and scowled at the floor, while the fourth, a slender man with a beard, whispered to his tall, slim companion.

"Answer me," El Chavo demanded. "Tell me who you are or by heaven . . . I've already got two prisoners to execute. What difference does it make if I eliminate five more?"

"What right does a man like you have to eliminate anyone?" the bearded man asked, his voice shrill and tinged with arrogance.

El Chavo laughed again. "What right? What right? Tell

him, *amigos,*" he cried, and gestured to the men in the
alcoves, who let loose a torrent of not-too-polite comments
and catcalls.

"Quite an intellectual group," the bearded man snapped.
"And I suppose you're that dreaded outlaw, El What's-His-
Name."

"*Oye,* Vicente," Benito called from his ledge. "What
happens when a smuggler murders the son of a local duke?
Do the smuggler's friends keep on protecting him?"

"Silence!" El Chavo shouted.

"Who was that?" the Gypsy demanded, peering into the
shadows. "It sounded like . . . my God, what's the village
saint doing in a smelly hole like this?"

"The same thing you are, Don Miguel. Facing immediate
execution."

"Ridiculous. These men can't touch me. My father would
have them blown off the earth."

"Would he?" El Chavo asked. "I wonder . . . does a duke
feel sympathy for a son who's a common thief? And who's
been caught prancing around the woods dressed like a
flamenco dancer?"

"Just a minute," the other slim Gypsy interrupted. "Since
it looks like I may be bargaining for my life, I insist we all
talk Castilian."

"Assuredly, my dear señor," El Chavo said with a smile.
"Assuming there's any bargaining to be done at all. Which I
sincerely doubt. The way I see it, you planned to steal those
statues but I got there first. So now you're here, and that's
that."

"We didn't just stumble on this place, you know," said
Don Miguel. "We were led here by one of your own—"

"Señor, please! For the love of heaven . . ." one of the
burly Gypsies cried out.

"Ay, *mi jefe,* that's Nacho," a smuggler called from an alcove. "You remember Nacho. He's the one who deserted the night that storm threatened to—"

"I remember Nacho," El Chavo said coldly. "And I must say, I don't feel much pleasure in seeing him again."

"Come on, Vicente, you don't want seven executions," Benito called from across the cave. "Not on the year's most important holiday. Besides, you've got the statues. So why not just abandon this cave and let the rest of us return to the *Romería?*"

"I hate to admit it, but the peasant has a point," said Don Miguel. "You can't possibly kill us all. Not if you hope to keep on living in this village."

"And if I don't?" El Chavo asked with a grin.

The tall, slim Gypsy pulled off his bandanna, revealing blond hair above his darkened face. "Whether anyone likes it or not, I propose an agreement. Namely: Don Diego's son will forget who stole the treasure if in return—"

"El What's-His-Name forgets Don Diego's son tried to steal it, too. Is that it?" the smuggler asked.

"Of course not," Don Miguel broke in. "What kind of an agreement is that? Nobody ends up with anything."

"Except me," El Chavo pointed out. "I end up with the statues, plus the son of Don Diego." He turned to his men. "Tie them up!"

"No, wait!" the nobleman cried as four smugglers came running out of an alcove. "You can't touch me. I'm the son of the duke of Última Alegría."

"You're a prisoner," El Chavo shouted. "And prisoners don't tell their captors what to do. Soriano! See that their bonds are tight, then put them on the ledge with the others."

•

As the running figure jumped down onto the deck, Concepción saw that it was a sturdy young man dressed, like the duke, as a fisherman. Then the light from the window shone on his face and she saw that it was the youngest son of Octavio Mora.

The duke pocketed his gun and stepped out from the shadows. "Ricardo, what's wrong?"

"This waiting," the young man panted. "My father thinks maybe we ought to—" He stopped, glared at Concepción. "What's she doing here?"

The duke laughed. "Don't be alarmed, my friend. I haven't taken leave of my senses. This is Benito Bazán's wife."

"His wife! What do we want with his wife? I thought—"

"Calm yourself, Ricardo," the duke said softly.

"People who don't live up to their agreements make me sick," the young man grumbled.

Concepción drew herself up. "Excuse me, señor, but if my husband agreed to take you and your father fishing, then had he not gone off after the thieves, my husband would have taken you and your father fishing."

"Indeed?" Ricardo asked, with a trace of sarcasm.

"Assuredly."

The duke laughed. "What spirit you display, Señora Bazán. And what loyalty. But what if I told you our trip had another purpose entirely?"

Concepción stiffened. Could the duke be talking about one of those shameless cruises where noblemen and women . . .

"I don't question my husband's decisions," she replied, "nor does he, in return, question mine."

"Admirable, admirable," chuckled the duke. "Then if you decided to use what you know about boats to—"

"Never, señor."

"Not even if I told you ours was an errand of mercy?"
She grunted.

"Or that by running after his treasure, Benito may have sentenced Octavio Mora and his family to death?"

"What does she care?" Ricardo muttered.

Concepción raised her chin and squared her shoulders. "In Galicia, Don Ricardo, women, too, have a sense of honor. If my husband agreed to do something, believing this an errand of mercy, then tell me what he agreed to do, and if I'm at all able, I'll do it for him."

"Magnificent!" cried Don Diego.

"Absurd," said Don Ricardo. "In a situation like this, what can a woman—"

"A *gallega,*" Concepción corrected him.

"I repeat, what can a woman—"

"She can try," said Don Diego, "the same as anyone."

He smiled, laid a hand on the young man's shoulder. "Come now, Ricardo. I'm as interested in getting there alive as you are. And in getting home in the same condition. So please . . . at this point we don't have a choice."

"No," Ricardo sighed, "I don't suppose we do."

"But you don't have to say that to your father and mother."

"No, I guess I don't."

"Good. Then tell them to finish their packing and get down here right away. In the meantime I'll tell Señora Bazán how she can fulfill her husband's obligation, gain a duke's respect, and in the process, earn for herself a fishing boat."


"Mitsubishi!"

"Hitachi!"

The trapdoor opened, and El Bruto clomped down the

steps, followed by a dozen men carrying gas masks.

"*Oyen amigos,* we're back," he shouted. "Not that we didn't have them nipping at our heels all the way to—" He stopped. Nodded toward the lineup on the ledge. "What's going on?"

"Unexpected guests," El Chavo replied.

"Oh, ho," boomed the man with the scar. "And I see my friend Benito Bazán over there, too. Wonderful! We'll get rid of all our problems at once." He laughed, slapped himself on the thigh. "*Vivan los célticos!*"

El Chavo regarded his assistant coldly. "I said nobody was to drink."

"And I say the statues are home at last. *Vivan los célticos.*"

"Soriano! Prepare a giant urn of coffee."

"Coffee!" thundered El Bruto. "A man doesn't execute one, two, three, four, five, six, SEVEN clowns on a bellyful of coffee."

There was a tense silence, broken at last by El Chavo. "Who said anything about executions?"

"I did," El Bruto declared. "It's time. More than time."

"I see."

"My men and I are tired of all this softness, aren't we, *muchachos?*"

The men who'd just entered looked at one another and shuffled their feet.

"The time has come to prove we're not a band of book-reading sissies. Right, *muchachos?*"

Some mumbled words. More shuffling. A few nervous coughs.

El Chavo turned on his heel and walked slowly to the pagan altar. There, he stood absolutely still, staring down at the great stone slab. Then, slowly, dramatically, he raised his head and turned to face the silent, expectant group.

"This is my cave," he said. "My cave and my band. Anyone who would like to dispute those facts, step forward and tell me so to my face."

Silence.

"All right," El Chavo went on, "since that's understood, let me state our position again: if in our daily work we can achieve an objective without bloodshed, then we shall achieve that objective without bloodshed. Do I make myself clear?"

"*Sí, mi jefe,*" mumbled the group.

"Bruto?"

Growling under his breath, the husky man stalked to the largest of the alcoves, where a coffee urn perked at him accusingly.

"Bruto?" El Chavo repeated.

"*Sí, mi jefe,*" he muttered over his shoulder.

"All right, then. And the next time I turn toward that table, I want to see you and your men holding coffee mugs. Understood?" Without waiting for a response, El Chavo walked toward the ledge. "Are the prisoners secure?"

"*Sí, mi jefe,*" said the man who was guarding them.

"Everyone comfortable?" the smuggler asked with a smile.

Benito grunted, wondering how a man could talk about killing seven innocent prisoners one minute and the next warn his men about avoiding bloodshed. It didn't make sense.

"That was quite a power struggle we just witnessed," said the blond Gypsy, Erik Frostmann. "You should be more careful, Chavo. We prisoners might turn that to our advantage."

"What do you propose we do?" asked Don Miguel. "Get this outlaw and his pet beast to start fighting, then try to—"

"As usual, you missed my point entirely," said Erik.

"What I was saying—subtly, I admit—was that this gentleman doesn't seem to realize we're worthy of more attention. To be specific, that he and I are in an excellent position to bargain."

Benito snorted. "If you ask me, a man tied hand and foot is in a poor position to do anything about anything."

Erik shot Benito a very dirty look. "Can we discuss this in private?" he asked the smuggler.

El Chavo grinned and shook his head. "I wouldn't dream of entering any agreement without the sage advice of Benito Bazán."

"You people do stick together, don't you?" murmured Don Miguel.

"We people?" El Chavo frowned and looked away. "Yes, I suppose when it comes down to it, we do."

"All right, then, here's my proposition," Erik said irritably. "You have some merchandise that might prove difficult to sell. I have a buyer free of embarrassing questions."

El Chavo smiled. "In other words, I spare your life, you introduce me to a middleman."

"Not at all. This is a bona fide collector. For him, money isn't the object."

"And for you?"

"You must agree, with an item so rare, a man like yourself would have to pay a commission to someone."

"True. But if possible, someone I could trust."

"Who could be more trustworthy than someone dependent on you for his life?"

"True again."

"And where a man of business, like Erik, could introduce you to a buyer," Don Miguel put in, "a member of the nobility could cause some, shall we say, embarrassing notations to be removed from a person's records."

"Thus ensuring him a trouble-free old age," El Chavo said.

"Precisely," the nobleman agreed.

"I don't believe it," said Benito. "Before my eyes Vicente Rodríguez has become a man who condemns the poor to death while bargaining with the rich and the powerful."

"Benito, please," the smuggler sighed. "Don't turn this into something political."

"Since when is asking to remain alive political?"

"Don't cross me, Benito. I warn you."

"If you're willing to hear their propositions, you should be willing to hear mine."

"Which is?"

"First, if you must sell the statues, sell them to Don Diego."

"Ha. Even you refused to do that."

"But for a good reason, Vicente. And I still intended to . . . to do what I'd promised. Though God knows what's going to happen to the poor man now."

"You're babbling, my friend," El Chavo said, and turned back to Erik Frostmann. "Tell me, this buyer of yours, when can I meet him?"

"Tonight if you like. He's waiting on his yacht. With two of his men ready to take me there in a speedboat."

"Assuming they can avoid a certain gunboat my son saw farther down the coast," Benito muttered.

"If you're implying the trip might be dangerous," El Chavo said, "may I remind you that for forty years I've successfully avoided any boat I didn't wish to encounter."

"And robbed those you did."

"Business is business, as they say in America."

"There, your grace, you see," Benito cried, turning eagerly to Don Miguel. "This man's been robbing boats for over forty years. Do you honestly think he'll leave those statues on the yacht and go home with a few pesetas?"

"How about a few million pounds?" Erik Frostmann asked dryly.

"For a king's ransom, El Chavo wouldn't leave a boat if she had anything of value aboard her. I think he's planning to—"

"Put a gag on that man!" El Chavo shouted.

"No, Vicente. Wait! I'm the one you should do business with. Me, Benito Bazán. A man you can—*mmmphfffff!!*"

# chapter 28 🌺🌺

While Benito breathed heavily through his nose, and El Bruto poured whiskey into his coffee mug, across the country in Madrid, General Agosto Tardesillas Gómez, clad in a brocade dressing gown, nodded curtly to his valet and strode to the telephone. It being nine o'clock, and the general being about to pick up his mistress for an early dinner at the Casa Botín, the last thing he wanted was an urgent call from the ministry.

"*Diga,*" he shouted into the transmitter. Then sank into the leather chair behind his desk. "What do you mean the house is empty? Where are they?"

A crackle on the line.

"And where in the name of God is that?"

Another crackle.

"I see. And he went there to give a speech?"

As he listened to the answer, the general drummed on the desk. This was serious. A man under investigation flying to Galicia, while in Madrid an informant appears with news of a journal that spanned forty years of political history. That named names, revealed opinions—not just of Mora but of other influential men who for years had seemingly supported the "bunker." There was no doubt: if such a journal existed, it had to be examined by the government.

"He has to be brought back," the general shouted. "Do you have any idea how the escape of a man like that could inspire the opposition? Notify the village mayor."

More crackling.

"What do you mean the line is down? Surely there's more than one. This is the twentieth century."

The crackling grew louder.

"Incredible," breathed the general, and sagged in his chair, all hope of a sensuous evening drifting out the window with the smoke from his cigarette. "Well, call Pontevedra. La Coruña. Anywhere. Tell whoever you reach to get someone there fast.

"What? Of course tonight. Have you looked at a map? That godforsaken place is on a *ría* that leads to the Atlantic Ocean."

# chapter 29 ✿✿✿✿

Was there anything she should be doing, Concepción wondered, except sitting at the small, fold-down table, watching the moon shimmering on the water?

So far, there didn't seem to be any reason for her to be on this boat at all. The duke and Mora's two sons were taking turns at the wheel; Don Octavio and Doña Ana were talking softly on the lower bunk; and except for an occasional cluster of fishing boats, the firth seemed peaceful and deserted. Had she done right, agreeing to make this journey? Even now Benito might be lying in some ditch, calling out to her.

*Mi madre,* where did such thoughts come from, she asked herself, and to raise her spirits, turned from the waves and considered again the changes that had been made in Paco's old cabin. First off, the whole place seemed much larger than she remembered. Then there were all the additions: a shiny new wheel; a built-in cabinet beneath the forward window; an upper and lower bunk; a combination stove, sink, and refrigerator; a tiny room with a toilet. By heaven, on a boat like this a person could sail all the way to America, not just to that place Don Diego had showed her on the chart, a small island near where the Firth of Pontevedra widened to meet the Atlantic Ocean.

Remembering that chart, and what the duke had told her about the reason for this trip, Concepción looked at the white-haired man at the wheel, noticing as if for the first time the bony body, the thinning hair, the almost transparent skin. The duke was an old man, she thought, yet there he was, putting his beliefs on the line, risking capture along with Octavio Mora. Poor Don Diego, so many griefs he'd suffered over the years. The death of his wife, his eldest son . . . and, in many ways, his youngest one as well. Strange to think she could feel pity for a duke. Or for a family as rich as the Moras, she thought, gazing now at the somber couple sitting side by side on the lower bunk. What was it like to give up your house, your friends, even the country where you were born? Yet by being on this boat, Concepción was putting her beliefs on the line, too, she thought, aware of an unfamiliar weight resting atop her thigh, knowing if she put her hand in her pocket, her fingers would touch that smooth, deadly metal. If anything went wrong, could she possibly do what Don Diego had told her? Release the catch, take careful aim, squeeze the trigger . . .

"Perhaps it would be well to eat," Don Diego called over his shoulder. "Later on, should someone repair those telephone lines, it might not be so convenient."

"You're probably right," said Doña Ana, "but I, for one, couldn't touch a thing."

"Nor could I," her husband agreed, "though I imagine our sons could. I'll go tell them," he said, and rising from the bunk, crossed the cabin and went out onto the deck.

Sensing it was her duty to unpack the basket Don Diego's housekeeper had brought to the dock, Concepción lifted it to the table and looked inside. *Bien.* The woman had done well. Fresh crabs. Wine. Bread. Cheese. Fruit. Not that Concepción had any appetite, but when the others were through, it might be well to force down a little something.

Guessing that the dishes and silver were in the cabinet over the stove, she hurried over, took out what was needed, and set the table. Then, standing to one side, she watched Don Ricardo heap his plate, fill his glass, and start for the door.

"What about your brother?" Don Octavio called after him.

"Jaime's keeping watch with the binoculars," Ricardo called back. "He's not sure, but he thinks somebody might be following us."

"Who?" barked Don Diego, turning from the wheel. "And why didn't you tell me?"

Ricardo looked embarrassed. "We didn't want anyone to get upset until we were absolutely sure, but, well, Jaime thinks it may be your mayor's gunboat."

In the moonlit oak grove, what looked like a circular patch of leaves and twigs slowly began to move, one rim pivoting while the other rose to a point ninety degrees above the ground. At once a dark figure carrying a shielded flashlight in one hand and a silenced revolver in the other came out of the earth, scanned the shadowy woods, and apparently satisfied with what he'd seen, turned and called down to his companions.

Out they came, single file: two men with guns; seven with their hands tied behind their backs. Then yet another man with a gun—a man who ordered the trapdoor closed, the gunmen to shoot anyone who made a suspicious move, the prisoners to thank God they wouldn't be spending their final hours in a cave with thirty restless men, and all of them to fall in line and follow him down to the firth.

Useless to try to make a run for it, Benito decided as, following a smuggler named Carlos, he darted across the highway and set off on a trail through the pine trees. His only hope was that El Chavo meant what he'd said about avoiding bloodshed. That when he and his two Gypsy partners went off to the yacht, Benito and the three other Gypsies could overpower their guards, steal their weapons, and together with Paco run off into the moonlight. In the meantime, shoulders sagging, arms aching, he started down a zigzag trail to the beach, then plodded along the sand to where two men with rifles greeted El Chavo with a military salute.

"*Buenas noches, mi jefe.*"

"'*Noches.* Take these four and lock them in the hut," their leader barked, pointing out Paco and the three burly Gypsies. "The rest of us will be leaving in the launch."

"And me?" Benito asked.

"I just said . . . the rest of us will be leaving in the launch."

"But he's a prisoner," Erik Frostmann protested.

"And what are you?" El Chavo asked. "Besides, didn't I tell you I wouldn't enter any agreement without the sage advice of Benito Bazán?"

"Yes, but he has no right out there."

"No right!" Benito cried. "Whose treasure are you—"

"Silence!" El Chavo commanded. "I'm the one who decides who goes and who doesn't. So, by God, if I say Benito goes with us, Benito goes with us. El Chavo doesn't have to justify himself to any prisoner. El Chavo doesn't have to justify himself to anyone!"

Ay, what misery, Benito thought as, huddled in a rancid borrowed pullover whose sleeves barely came down to his wrists, he bounced across the waves, wondering why El Chavo insisted he go with them to the yacht. A form of torture, perhaps. Before tossing him into the waves or handing him over to El Bruto. Ay, if only Benito hadn't tried to be such a hero. He could have waited until the police and the army came back to the meadow, led them to the cave, and that would have been that. But no, he had to go galloping off on his own. And now poor Paco was shivering in a hut, and the statues were doomed again to be sold to a friend of Erik Frostmann.

Shuddering at the thought of losing them, as well as from the chill wind and the possibility of being killed as soon as the buyer sailed away, Benito turned his head and looked back over his shoulder, hoping for a glimpse of the mayor's gunboat. Where were those accursed fools? Surely if any boat looked suspicious, this one did. A powerful motor. Seven men. No sign of any fishing gear. All Benito would have to do would be point at El Chavo's knapsack, accuse him of being a thief, and—*qué maravilla!*—once again Benito would be a hero, saving the golden figures, capturing El Chavo, rescuing Paco Camino . . . Then it struck him: the mayor's men would never stop what, to them, must be a well-known member of the smuggler's fleet. Not if their employer hoped to keep wine, cigars, and God knew what else flowing across the desk of that second-floor office.

Because the yacht was bobbing lazily at anchor, her sails had been furled and lanterns lit both on deck and inside the cabin. Benito drew in his breath. Never, not even in La Coruña, had he seen a boat such as this. She was magnificent, absolutely magnificent. Eyes wide, he looked from one end of the sleek white hull to the other. Then, under his breath, tried to pronounce the words on the nearest life preserver: *The Gaylife. Lyme Regis.*

The smuggler Soriano cut the power, and as the launch drifted alongside, Erik Frostmann cupped his hands around his mouth and hallooed a greeting. Within seconds, a man in immaculate white trousers, blue blazer, and peaked white cap approached the teak-and-chrome railing and shouted back at him.

El Chavo nudged his Danish prisoner in the ribs. "Tell them they must give their guns to Soriano or the rest of us shall refuse to come aboard."

"Give up their guns?" Erik laughed. "You must be kidding."

"Try me. Otherwise, tell them Soriano will bring up a waterproof box, and when we leave, they'll be free to haul it out of the water."

"But that's—"

"Tell them!"

While Erik did as he was told, the smuggler turned to his men. "Soriano," he said, "you have the submachine gun?"

"Sí, mi jefe."

"Carlos and Eduardo, you have the grenades and flame-throwers?"

"Sí, mi jefe."

"Then, as usual, Soriano goes up and you two stay here."

"And him?" Carlos asked, jerking a thumb at Benito.

"Him?" El Chavo smiled and nodded to the rope ladder being thrown over the side of the yacht by two men in striped jerseys. "Benito's my special guest. He's going to go up first, so if there's any trouble, Soriano will have something to hide behind."

As Benito went up the ladder to the *Gaylife,* Concepción sat in the cabin of *La Mariposa,* absently chewing a bite of apple as she worried about both him and herself. Suddenly the door opened and Don Ricardo poked in his head.

"It's the gunboat, all right," he shouted. "And they're picking up speed."

"Damn!" said the duke. "How long have we got?"

"Ten, fifteen minutes."

"All right, you two keep watch. I'll see to your father and mother."

"Right," said Ricardo, ducked back, and slammed the door.

"Now what?" asked Don Octavio. "Can we go faster? Outrun them?"

The duke shook his head. "They've got guns. Radios. Friends all along the coast. Damn!" he repeated. "With police from anywhere else we could do what we'd planned: keep the women inside and pretend the rest of us were fishermen."

"Maybe it's not as bad as we think," Mora suggested. "Maybe they're stopping everyone."

"One sight of their duke at the wheel of a fishing boat and they'll know something isn't what it should be."

"I have it," Don Octavio cried. "We Moras will hide while you and Señora Bazán pretend you're returning the boat to Las Palomillas."

Don Diego looked at him in amazement. "Why would Señora Bazán be doing that? Or I, for that matter?"

"God knows," Mora breathed, his shoulders slumping. "I just thought we had to do something."

"Amen," said the duke, "and the first thing is, hide you and Ana. Maybe out on deck. We could cover you with tarpaulins."

"Excuse me, your grace," Concepción put in, "but wouldn't it be easier for them to slip in that cabinet under the window? Unless, of course, it's got shelves in it . . . or isn't big enough," she finished lamely.

"Of course it's big enough," the duke exclaimed. "Why didn't I think of that?" And putting the wheel on automatic control, slid back the door, knelt down, and began pulling out blankets and extra clothing.

"Surely we can't both get in there," Doña Ana gasped as, standing beside the duke, she surveyed the rapidly emptying space.

"It'll be tight," Don Diego agreed, "but I'll leave the door slightly open so you'll be sure to get enough air."

"It isn't air I'm concerned with," said Doña Ana. "Look at Octavio's height. And my width."

"You can do it. You have to," snapped Don Diego, then called over his shoulder, "Señora Bazán. Tell Jaime and Ricardo to remain on deck and pretend to be fishermen. Tell them if the men come on board to stay in the shadows and say as little as possible."

Glad to be of help, Concepción ran from the cabin, delivered the duke's instructions, glanced at the oncoming boat, shuddered, and went back. The Moras were nowhere to be seen, but in front of the built-in cabinet Don Diego was bent over double, scooping up an armload of clothing and blankets. Suddenly it struck Concepción there were other things to put away, too, and darting to the table, she piled up the unused plates and ran with them back to the cupboard.

"Ay, and the food," she exclaimed, returning to the table. "I have to put away all this food. It looks like we've been having a party."

"Or an orgy," panted the duke, flinging another bundle into the shadows of the upper bunk. "Which brings up something else," he said, gasping for breath as he turned to face her. "What are we going to do about you and me? We can't just . . . Wait a minute. What Octavio said about the two of us sailing to Las Palomillas . . ."

Stroking his chin, the duke looked thoughtfully at

220

Concepción, then around the messy cabin. "Yes, that's it," he murmured. Strode to the door and told Jaime to man the auxiliary controls.

"And don't come in," he added. "Señora Bazán and I are going to be busy with other things."

He closed the door and pulled off his thick black sweater.

"All right, señora, off with that shawl. Then the skirt, blouse, whatever else—"

"Ay, señor! Surely you're not thinking of . . ."

The duke unzipped his trousers. "For the good of your country, Señora Bazán, not to mention the life of the Moras, please, take off that clothing."

"Ay, Don Diego," she wailed as the skinny old duke, in underwear and shorts, flipped back the covers and crawled into the lower bunk.

"What are you doing?" he cried, pulling up the covers. "Don't just stand there. Undress and come in. Now, woman, now!"

# chapter 30

Wedged in a white wicker chair, Benito shifted his stubby fingers, hoping to get a better grip on the flimsy stem of his champagne glass. Champagne. Pink carpeting. Plants dangling over one's head. What kind of a boat was this? Nothing was as it should be. But when he looked at the man in the satin trousers and flowered kimono sitting on the purple couch across from him, he thought he knew why. Though well over sixty, the captain had skin that was as soft and pink as that on a rich man's baby. Then there was the curly red hair, the pouting lips, the spidery fingers that would soon be closing around the laughing lovers.

Benito shuddered and looked down at his little friends, gleefully mating on the glass-topped coffee table. Ay, if only there was something he could do. Better for El Chavo to take possession than a man who giggled at other men like a milkmaid.

"A hundred thousand pounds, that's as high as I shall go," the captain declared in precise, lisping Castilian.

Erik snorted. "My dear Alex, are you aware Norton Simon paid nine hundred thousand dollars for the *Shivapuram Nataraja?*"

"And are you aware before any museum would display it, he had to agree that in ten years' time he'd return it to India?"

"You're not concerned with displaying these statues in a museum, and you know it."

"True. And I'm not Norton Simon, either."

"Also true," Erik agreed. "But you're not exactly a pauper. And whatever you offer, I have to share with the gentleman on my left." He smiled at El Chavo, who grunted as he reached in the pocket of his windbreaker for a cigar.

"Oh, must you?" Alex asked, pouting. "It takes days to get that awful smell out of my draperies."

El Chavo put back the cigar, crossed his legs, and glared down at the statues.

"That's interesting, you know, Erik," Don Miguel said softly. "I mean what you said about sharing your profits with

El Chavo. Somehow I thought I was a partner in this, too."

"All right, if you have to quibble," Erik snapped, "so there are three of us. All the more reason for demanding a higher price."

The baby-skinned man picked up the little figures, pulled them apart, then with appraising eyes fitted them back together again. "Alas," he sighed "who knows the true value of this perverted pair? Certainly I don't. But I do know that, unlike the *Nataraja,* they're not an object of worship for a hundred million people. In fact, when it comes to the subject matter, I, for one, find them frankly repulsive." And with a grimace of distaste, set the interlocked pair back on the coffee table.

"You think if you disparage the merchandise, we'll lower our price," Erik observed, "but we won't."

"Oh, won't you? I wonder . . ." Alex snapped his fingers, and the man in the blue jacket stepped forward to fill the champagne glasses.

Benito stared down at the bubbly gold liquid, wondering how much longer he was going to have to sit there listening to all the nipping and pecking. Wondering, too, if there were some way he could convince the captain not to buy . . .

"They're not real gold, you know," he muttered.

"What?" The man in the kimono raised his plucked red eyebrows. "Why, of course they are. You can tell that just by looking at them."

"And they're not antique, either," Benito protested. "At least, not so antique as you think they are."

"Not Celtic? Ridiculous. Look at those oversized noses. The woman's necklace. That pleated skirt." He frowned, turned to Erik Frostmann. "Say, who is this man, anyway?"

"Me?" Benito smiled. "I'm the statues' owner."

"What!"

"That's nonsense," Erik said. "He's not the owner, we are."

"You mean I am," El Chavo corrected him.

"True, true," Erik went on, "the important thing, we have the right to sell and Alex has the right to buy."

"Or not buy," Alex simpered.

"That's right, señor," Benito broke in. "Don't buy. The figures aren't worth it."

"That's enough, Benito," El Chavo warned him. "I won't have you—"

"Then why did you bring him?" Erik demanded.

"That's my affair," El Chavo shot back.

"I told you," sighed Don Miguel. "These people stick together."

"Please, please." Alex raised his pudgy pink palms. "All this shouting. Surrendering my guns to that beast on the deck." He shivered. "Really, it's all very distressing."

"Then let's finish our business and be done with it," El Chavo said brusquely. "You heard our price. Take it or leave it."

"My, my," the captain cooed, hand to his throat. "Give a man a minute to think . . ."

Fighting the urge to dive across the table and throttle that fleshy pink throat, Benito crossed his arms and glared at the man in the flowered kimono. Then, unable to bear the anguish, looked down at the glass-topped table, where in the golden glow of the lamps his beloved friends delighted in their lusty communion. He swallowed, looked up to see Don Miguel nervously stroking his beard, Erik Frostmann glowering at El Chavo, El Chavo scowling at the pensive, sipping captain. Aching with loss, Benito closed his eyes. The boat was rocking gently, and waves slapped against the hull. Waves against the hull . . . a sound he'd dreamed he'd be hearing night after night. And now *La Mariposa* was gone. As were the golden statues . . .

"No," he breathed and opened his eyes. Across the cabin a painting vibrated with random splashes of color. Beside it stood the statue of a naked man, missing his head, one arm, and both legs below the knees. Soon, when the captain paid the agreed-upon price, another work of art would be displayed along that bulkhead. On a pedestal, no doubt, the lovers being so small . . .

"No," he repeated, setting his fragile glass down on the coffee table.

"NO!" he shouted. "They're mine! You have no right to them!"

Leaping from his chair, he swept the statues into their box, put the box under his arm, and ran for the door.

"Wait! Stop! Come back here," Alex shrieked as the others sprang to their feet and raced from the cabin.

On deck a gaping Soriano confronted Benito with the submachine gun.

Benito panicked. Stopped. Dashed to the railing.

"Don't shoot!" El Chavo shouted.

*"Vivan los célticos!"* Benito cried, and threw a leg over the railing.

"Shall I graze him, *mi jefe?*" Soriano implored.

"No, leave him to me," El Chavo replied, moving across the deck, pistol in hand.

"Is this why you brought him?" Erik Frostmann demanded. "So you could get control of everything?"

"You call this control?" El Chavo shouted, approaching the man at the rail as though he were a vicious wild animal.

"Come on, Benito. You can't go down in that launch. My men will massacre you."

"You want us to kill him now, *mi jefe?*" a voice called from below.

"No," El Chavo repeated. "Leave him to me."

Leg over the rail, Benito turned his head. "Shoot me, Vicente, if you must. Or have Soriano do it. But I warn you, before I die I'll throw the golden couple into the sea."

"I thought you loved them so much," sneered Erik.

"Better surrounded by sharks than people like you."

"Come on, *amigo,*" El Chavo urged. "Hand me that box and I swear you, too, will get a share of the profits."

"Money? What do I want with money? These figures belong to the citizens of Amor Milagroso."

"He's insane," said Don Miguel. "He really believes that."

"So what are you going to do?" El Chavo asked. "By God, you can't sit on that rail forever."

"Nor can you stand here arguing," cried the man in the blue jacket, and with a quick kick, knocked the pistol from the smuggler's one good hand.

Quick as a cat, Erik Frostmann dived to the deck and retrieved it. "Now," he said, scrambling to his feet, "now we'll see who gives the orders around here." He aimed the gun at El Chavo. "Tell that man of yours to throw down his weapon or, by heaven, you'll never again tell anybody anything."

Nursing his injured hand, El Chavo turned to Soriano and told him to do what the man said.

"But *mi jefe,* Carlos and Eduardo—"

"Soriano!"

Muttering under his breath, the smuggler dropped the submachine gun, and the man in the blue jacket ran forward, picked it up, and aimed it at El Chavo.

"There, that's better," said Erik, and walked toward Benito. "Now, give me that box."

"No," Benito said, cradling it in his arms like a baby.

"I warn you," Erik snapped, "I'm not afraid to kill like this flower you call an outlaw."

"Shoot and the statues go over the side."

"Miguel!" Erik barked. "Take it away from him."

"But didn't you hear?" asked Don Miguel. "He said he'd—"

"Are you my partner or aren't you?"

"Of course I am, but—"

"Then get that box or our relationship is over. Do you understand? Get it or get out."

"Now, see here, Erik, just because—"

"Oh, good. An argument between lovers," a woman called out in English.

Erik wheeled, and El Chavo, without a second's hesitation, dived forward and knocked him to the deck. There was a brief struggle, then El Chavo scrambled to his feet, once again in possession of his gun.

"Carlos! Eduardo!" the smuggler yelled. "Ready with those grenades and flamethrowers."

"Oooohhh, does that mean we'll have to take to the lifeboats?" asked Iris Duveaux, who, in a fur wrap and filmy green dress, came strolling down the deck, carrying a champagne glass. "What's going on? Is this some kind of war?"

"Now, *mi jefe,* now?" a voice called from the launch.

"Thirty seconds," El Chavo called back. Then turned to the railing. "All right, Benito. Down in the boat."

"No," Erik screamed, gazing wild-eyed at the man in the blue jacket. "Don't just stand there. Shoot!"

"My, it's a lovely night," said Alex, sauntering toward the

group, a bottle in one hand, a glass of champagne in the other.

"Alex, what are you doing?" Erik hollered in English. "Why don't you order your man to shoot?"

The baby-skinned man pivoted on a pale blue sandal. "And get stains on my lovely teak deck?"

"Those statues are worth a fortune," Erik wailed.

"So is my freedom," said Alex. "From what I was told last week in Cádiz, one more incident aboard this boat and as far as Spain is concerned I'm persona non grata."

"Cádiz was a drag," Iris declared, and walking to the railing, looked up at Benito with wide, mascaraed eyes. "Ah, Señor Bazán. *Buenas noches.*"

Still straddling the railing, Benito looked down at her in amazement. "The señora has been on this boat all the time?"

"*Sí.* And you know what brought me out of my cabin? I heard you giving the—what did you call it?—Amor Milagroso war cry."

"Bitch," Erik muttered in English. "What did you do? Phone Alex from the villa?"

Iris turned, earrings jangling. "A woman has to think of her future. And you will admit, working for him gives me certain advantages." She gestured around the yacht. "Besides," she added, "I didn't like playing decoy."

"You were as eager to—"

"Now, *mi jefe,* now?"

"Fifteen seconds," El Chavo barked. "Benito, for God's sake, what are you waiting for?"

"He thinks he might get laid," Erik yelled. Then added in English, "Iris is good at that."

"Prick!" she cried. "Who put me up to it?"

"You weren't asked to seduce him. Just keep him out of our hair until Nacho and his men—"

"Ten seconds," El Chavo said. "Benito, start down the ladder."

"Alex," Erik wailed, "please . . ."

"Please what?" Alex asked. "Our man has a gun; their man has a gun. They've also got grenades and flamethrowers. Plus a crazy peasant who says if anyone makes a move he'll throw the statues into the sea. So what can I do?" He burped. "Unless I call the peasant's bluff. That might be amusing."

"No," Iris said softly, "let Benito have them."

"Anything to keep them away from me, is that it?" Erik snarled.

She smiled. "That's it, cookie."

"I give up," Erik said with a sigh. "You and Alex are just going to stand there. Wave good-bye to millions of dollars."

"On the contrary," said Alex. "As soon as this riffraff is out of the way, we're sailing to where we can get millions and millions. From a sheik or shah or something who's dying to sell a solid gold you-know-what. From what I hear, the thing is two feet tall and makes that dreary Celtic pair look like a geegaw from Brighton."

"Hmmmm, solid gold . . ." Erik muttered.

"Uh-huh," Alex agreed. "Interested?"

"Could be. God knows, there's nothing in Spain to hold me."

"That's right," said Don Miguel, heading for the ladder. "Nothing and nobody . . ."

# chapter 31

Hugging the carved wooden box to his chest, a dazed Benito Bazán sat in the middle seat of the launch, staring at the moonlit waves but seeing only the yacht, Erik Frostmann, pistols, machine guns. He twitched, held the box even tighter, prayed he wouldn't get sick.

"Here, you have greater need of this than I do," said Don Miguel, and spread his borrowed windbreaker over Benito's shivering shoulders.

Benito nodded and managed to produce a tentative smile. The jacket felt good but did nothing to stop the shakes, which were caused not by the cold but by having looked death in the face and lived to tell of it. And for what? To lose the statues and probably confront yet another gun the instant the launch hit the beach . . .

"Are you all right?" the nobleman asked, laying an anxious hand on Benito's forearm.

"*Sí, sí . . .*"

"Good, because before we get back, there's something I'd like to tell you."

He paused, glanced at El Chavo's back, then moved closer to Benito and lowered his voice.

"This is hard for me to say," he began, "but back on the yacht, well, I have to admit I felt terribly proud of you."

Benito grunted. Proud? Of a man who'd risked all and gained nothing . . .

"No, seriously," the nobleman went on. "And even before that, back in the meadow. You see, there I was in these ridiculous clothes, peering through the bushes, waiting my chance to become a thief. And suddenly there was the mayor, saying Benito Bazán wasn't going to sell. And there were your friends, lifting you to their shoulders. I don't know . . . all at once I felt rather sick."

"So did I," Benito muttered, "so did I."

"I remember looking through the leaves at my father, thinking there'd be no crowd cheering *me* that afternoon. I'd been about to do what I'd always done—sadden and disappoint him. Strange, I'd never really seen it from his point of view before. All I'd seen was my own hurt, my own disappointment when he gave his love to my brother Rodrigo. Then when Rodrigo was killed and all my father had left was me . . ."

His fingers tightened on Benito's arm. "I know it's crazy, but I want to make it up to him, Benito, I really do. Only now there isn't any more time."

"Bah. El Chavo's not going to kill us."

"He's not?"

"Didn't he say in the cave he didn't want any bloodshed?"

"But he's the 'Terror of the Coast.' "

"Only to those who don't really know him," Benito announced, surprised at his sudden insight.

The nobleman brightened. "Then there's still hope. I mean, I know I can never be what my father wants—a son who will give him a grandson—but surely there's something I can do to make him proud of me, isn't there, Benito? Isn't there?"

"Of course, of course . . ."

Following his own train of thought, wondering where it was about to lead him.

The motor sputtered and coughed.

Benito stirred. Opened his eyes. Around the launch was nothing but a chill gray mist. Then from out of this nothingness, a shout:

"You in the boat! Advance and be recognized!"

Benito peered into the fog. Saw vague forms. The dim outline of a dock.

"I thought you said this place would be deserted," El Chavo called over his shoulder.

"It should be," Don Miguel called back.

"Yes? Well, it isn't. Look."

"The *Guardia*," gasped Don Miguel. "What are they—"

"God only knows. Quick, Soriano! Back to the open water."

"You in the boat," the voice bellowed again. "Ten seconds or we use our machine gun."

"We're coming, we're coming," El Chavo shouted. Told Soriano to pull up along the dock, and everyone to remember they were fishermen from another town, bringing Don Miguel home from the *Romería*.

So that was where they were, Benito thought, the duke's private cove. Which meant Don Miguel was being set free. Another clue El Chavo wasn't the killer he made himself out to be.

The launch slowed and a policeman threw down a line while two *Guardias* pointed to an iron ladder. Don Miguel went up first, followed by Benito, El Chavo, and the three other smugglers. The nobleman immediately started talking with the *Guardias* while Benito looked down the dock and blinked. Who would have thought? Crowding this private pier were two more *Guardias*, seven local policemen, and thirty or forty villagers, still in their *Romería* clothes.

"Look, there's Don Miguel," a man called out.

"And Benito Bazán," shrieked a woman.

"*Oye*, Benito. Did you catch those accursed thieves?"

"Where are the lovers? Where are the lovers?"

"Here!" Benito yelled, and waved the wooden box. "*Vivan los célticos!*"

The villagers whooped and surged forward.

"Quiet!" shouted a *Guardia*.

"Keep back," hollered a policeman.

"We want the statues, we want the statues," the crowd began to chant.

"All right, back to the beach," the policeman yelled, and together with his colleagues started herding the villagers toward the shore.

Just then, the nobleman finished his conversation with the *Guardias* and turned to Benito and the smugglers.

"My friends," said Don Miguel, "these gentlemen want to know if when we were out on the firth we saw anything that looked suspicious."

"Suspicious?" El Chavo asked.

"You know, a boat running without lights, staying too close to the shore, that sort of thing."

El Chavo shrugged. "We saw nothing, did we, *amigos*?"

His men grunted and shook their heads, while Benito tucked the wooden box firmly into his armpit.

"That's what I told them," the nobleman said, "so maybe now they'll explain what they and all these people are doing on my father's dock."

"Your father's disappeared, Don Miguel," said one of the

local policemen. "As has the family of Octavio Mora."

Benito turned his head. Hallelujah. *La Mariposa* had sailed after all. But had the duke himself been forced to help Pepe lead the Moras to freedom?

"Disappeared," the nobleman cried. "What do you mean? Have they been kidnapped?"

"Hard to say, your grace," the policeman replied. "We heard from Madrid, Señor Mora wasn't what he appeared to be."

"You mean not really a member of the Cortes? Or that the man we met wasn't really Mora?"

"I don't know, your grace. All they told us—"

"All right, that's enough," the *Guardia* broke in. "Our orders are to patrol this dock and question everyone who enters this harbor. So if Señor Granflaqueza and his friends have nothing to report . . ."

The nobleman's face went red. "You dare to order—" He stopped, and lips firm, took El Chavo by the arm and led him farther along the dock. Benito followed, but the three smugglers, after a moment's hesitation, started down the ladder to the launch.

"That officious clod," muttered Don Miguel. "I don't know why we— But that's beside the point. What I want you to know is this: everything I saw and heard tonight has already been forgotten."

"That's strange," El Chavo said with a smile. "I, too, have suffered a sudden loss of memory. But not regarding a promise I made about sharing certain profits."

Don Miguel raised his eyebrows. "A Granflaqueza engage in buying and selling? Never," he announced. "Yet I must admit, when it comes to correcting a few errors on the public records . . ."

The smuggler bowed. "I'm sure your grace is a very able administrator."

"Which means my associates in the hut will regain their freedom?"

"You have my word."

"Paco, too, I hope," Benito muttered.

"Yes," the smuggler sighed. "Paco, too."

"Well, good-bye, then," said Don Miguel, thrusting out his hand. "And thanks to both of you for . . . for a lot of things."

"A strange man," Benito said as the slender figure started down the dock toward the villa. "I only hope, should the occasion demand, he'll be able to offer forgiveness as well as ask for it."

"You mean if his father and Mora have been off on some kind of spree?" El Chavo asked.

"That, or worse."

Below, in the launch, Soriano started the motor.

"There's our signal," El Chavo said, and gestured to Benito to precede him.

Benito shook his head. "Thanks, *amigo*. I think I'll stay here."

"Then give me that box."

"No."

"You dare . . ."

"Under the circumstances, yes."

"You know the minute you're alone my men will—"

"I wonder . . . would even the 'Terror of the Coast' willfully murder his partner?"

"Partner! When did that happen?"

"When you refused to pull that trigger."

"Ridiculous."

"Is it? I've been thinking. You don't need all that money. What would you do with it?"

"Buy things. Travel. Surround myself with beautiful women."

"Bah. You can do that now. What you need is adventure."

"At my age?"

"The adventure I'm talking about is becoming one of Amor Milagroso's leading citizens."

"Just as I thought. You've gone completely insane."

"Have I? Think. If the statues stay here, we'll have pilgrims coming from Orense, Zamora, maybe as far as Madrid."

"So?"

"So, we'll have to have hotels, restaurants, a steady supply of certain luxuries . . ."

"You mean you and I . . ." El Chavo frowned and rubbed the stubble on his chin. Then, walking to the ladder, told Soriano to go back to the beach and release the captive birds.

"All of them, *mi jefe?*"

"Yes, all of them. I'm staying here. I've got something to think about."

The boat roared off, and the smuggler and Benito started for the shore, where the crowd stood clustered at the end of the dock, waiting to greet the returning hero.

"See," Benito said, "these statues mean a lot to them."

"I'm a fool even to agree to talk about this," El Chavo said, reaching for a cigar. "I ought to let you go, bide my time . . ."

"You tried that, remember?"

"That's right, I did. Why, I'll never know."

"Maybe you looked on me as a friend."

"God in heaven!"

"Why else bring me to that yacht?"

The smuggler shrugged, then struck a match. "Didn't I tell you? A one-armed bandit is hard to control. Sometimes even by the one-armed bandit himself."

"Which means?"

"Maybe I didn't really want to sell to that buffoon in the bathrobe."

"You didn't know he was a buffoon when you started out."

"I knew he was a friend of Erik Frostmann."

"And I wasn't."

"No, I guess you were one of my own, as Don Miguel would say." He paused, blew out a cloud of smoke. "Even so, you're an embarrassment to me, Benito, you know that? My men couldn't understand why I didn't run down to that farm and kill you. What they didn't know . . . what nobody knows . . . is that El Chavo has never killed anyone."

"Ah," Benito said, not really surprised by the revelation. "And yet those wonderful tales of bodies in the woods. Even María del Carmen swears she saw—"

"Show an excitable young girl the blood of a rabbit and she'll swear she's witnessed a massacre."

"You mean each of your men thought the others were . . . wait. What's going on?" Pointing to the beach, where the villagers were running toward two approaching policemen.

"I don't know," said El Chavo, "let's go see."

Together they ran to the end of the dock, jumped down into the sand, and hurried to the group.

"What's wrong?" Benito panted.

"News from the village," a man called over his shoulder.

"What kind of news?" El Chavo demanded.

"They found the duke in the cabin of Paco's boat."

"Not only that," a woman added. "He was sharing his bed with Concepción Peralta de Bazán.'

# chapter 32

Warmed by a mug of cocoa thoughtfully provided by the duke's housekeeper, Benito walked to the end of the dock, nodded to the *Guardias,* and for what must have been the five-hundredth time since learning Concepción was aboard *La Mariposa,* peered out at the swirling gray mist.

It seemed strange, waiting on the shore for his wife, when for so many years she had been the one waiting there for him. He hadn't realized staring into a gray expanse could be so unsettling. Especially when the person staring had to pretend it wasn't disaster he was concerned about, but debauchery.

Finally, around eleven o'clock, Manolo pointed to a shadowy form emerging from what was left of the fog.

"Ay, *papá*! There she is!"

"Thank God," breathed Benito.

"My, she looks fine," sighed Paco Camino.

"In truth, she does," Benito agreed, relieved to find the boat didn't appear to have been damaged or shot at.

*La Mariposa* came alongside, the motor stopped, and a small, slender man came out of the cabin, dressed like a fisherman. Without a word he walked directly to the stern, picked up a line, then turned and surveyed the few remaining villagers.

"Bastard," muttered Paco. "What are you going to do, Benito? Jump down there and challenge him?"

Benito grunted, and knowing his friends were watching every move, pushed to the front of the group and stalked to the mooring post.

"Here, your grace," he shouted. "Throw your line to me."

"Ah, Benito, you're safe," Don Diego cried.

"And you, your grace? Did you enjoy your night of fishing? Or did the big one, as so often happens, escape the nets entirely?"

The duke smiled. "The big one has much to be thankful for. God was good; He gave him his freedom."

Tears welled in Benito's eyes. "And your crew? They are safe, too?"

"See for yourself."

Benito turned. Coming out of the cabin was Concepción, her face flushed, her *Romería* clothes rumpled. He swallowed, thinking never had she looked more lovely. Never had he felt so proud of her.

"*Oye, mujer,*" he croaked. "Welcome home."

"Ay, Benito," she began. Then hesitated, her eyes moving from one inquiring face to the next.

"So you've decided to become a fisherman," he said, reaching out a hand, his heart so filled with love he feared it was going to burst inside his rib cage.

"You're the fisherman, *hombre,*" she said, crossing the cluttered deck. "Especially now that you've got yourself a boat."

"No, *mujer,*" he said, helping her up onto the dock. "This boat belongs to you."

"Ay, Benito. What need have I for a fishing boat?"

"Or I?" he laughed, showing her the carved wooden box.

"We have the—? How did you—?"

He shrugged. "A man does what he must, and if God smiles on his efforts . . ."

"And on his wife's . . ."

"Assuredly, assuredly," he said, putting an arm around her waist. "Well, then, what do you say? Shall we give *La Mariposa* to Manolo?"

# epilogue

Some believe Amor Milagroso began to change the instant Benito took the box from the pagan altar. Others, when the male was united with the female. Who can say? Yet change the village did. Especially when the lovers became a national treasure and pilgrims from all over the world started flocking to Amor Milagroso to see what the zestful duo could do for them.

And today?

Today the Celtic lovers perform the act of love every hour on the hour in the beautifully lit grotto under the oak grove. For a while there was some question who actually owned that cave, but finally, the relevant parchments being so brittle, the entries in the relevant ledgers so faded, it was decided at a town meeting—now a village tradition—that the Peraltas and their neighbors, the Rabals (each of whom claimed their ancestors had purchased the land), should split the disputed territory as the pope once split the world: fifty-fifty. Thus, by an accident of geography, the Peraltas were named the cave's legal owners and the lovers gained a permanent home.

To see them, pilgrims pay a fee (which grows larger every year) at the gate to what was once the Peralta vineyard, follow a tanbark trail to the top of the hill (or take the funicular), pause perhaps at the wood-and-stone reception center under the oak trees, then fall in line, proceed to the open cement trapdoor, descend the broad stone staircase, inch across the vaulted chamber, and at last reach the eye-level wooden shaft which stands directly under the stained-glass skylight. There, they walk slowly around the lovers (joined or separated, depending on the time of day), then either remain in the grotto to see other items of interest (bits and pieces of the original wooden box, a hand-lettered placard, a sheepskin rain hat cut to reveal a secret inner pocket) or leave by the new wooden staircase under the glowing sign reading SALIDA.

Once outside, many pilgrims stroll down to what was once the Peralta farmhouse, where at moderate cost they can buy a typical Galician meal. These meals used to be cooked by women of the village, but today, what with the number of pilgrims and their level of sophistication, the food is prepared by an experienced restaurateur who, it is said, is thinking of selling his franchise to a well-known international snack shop.

Besides enjoying good food at reasonable prices, those pilgrims wise enough to have made reservations well in advance can proceed across the well-trimmed lawn to the stone building which once housed the Peralta livestock but has since been converted into a quaint, rustic hotel boasting handmade quilts, hand-woven rugs, and hand-painted pottery. (The fact that the latter comes from Andalucía seems

to disturb the average pilgrim not at all.) For obvious
reasons, this hotel, the *Posada de los Amantes,* or Lovers' Inn,
is extremely popular with honeymooners. In fact, during the
summer months it is almost impossible to reserve a room
there at all.

As well as being a mecca for tourists and pilgrims, the
shrine is also popular with the villagers. Sometimes they sit
beneath the oaks and chat with the garrulous old caretaker,
Paco Camino (whose son and grandson, home from Milan,
live in a cottage down near the harbor). Sometimes, when the
line is short, they go down into the cave and renew their
acquaintance with the golden couple. Entrance fees are not a
problem because many of the older residents have lifetime
passes. And even the young can get in if a good-natured
guard like Ignacio León or Andrés Rabal is on duty. Then
there are passes (issued as prizes for this and that), discounts,
and an occasional free day, so, as of now, even the poor have a
chance to see the treasure at some time.

The mayor, however, visits the statues at least once a
week—often with his young American wife. Not, he says, for
the reason everyone thinks, but to display his gratitude, the
shrine having been what finally put his village in the
guidebooks (an event he believed impossible after the traitor
Octavio Mora escaped from under the mayor's nose).

The village priest often visits the treasure, too. Not in his
official capacity, of course, but as a teacher of pagan my-
thology, bringing with him the men and women currently
enrolled in his popular night course.

In addition to these changes on the hilltop, things in the
village are different now, too. Every year more and more
citizens are becoming craftspersons, consigning their wares
either to a booth in the new central market or—if judged

artistic enough—to the wood-and-stone reception center under the oak trees. The mayor's wife has the final say on what is or is not artistic enough to be displayed at the latter location, and it was she who recently stopped an American entrepreneur from sending plastic copies of the lovers, which, he assured her, in America would soon be "as hot an item as Barbie and Ken."

The café, of course, is still the center of the village life. The old café, that is, not the glass-and-steel monstrosity near the harbor where tourists are invited to enjoy "the ever-changing vista of sea and of sky." In fact, once a month, after the town meeting, *El Gran Gaitero* is more alive than the mayor really likes, for when the debates are over and as much as possible has been done to preserve the quality of village life, reports and microphones are set aside, the wine flows, and the wainscoted room echoes with singing and dancing. Pilgrims who chance to witness one of these celebrations go away feeling especially privileged, as though, in addition to everything else, they've glimpsed the true spirit of this remarkable town named Miraculous Love.

And the man who brought about all these changes? He and his wife live quietly in the village, as do their sons, Antonio, José, and Manolo. From time to time, Benito goes fishing with Manolo on *La Mariposa,* but more often he, José, and Antonio (home permanently from Buenos Aires and report-edly courting the eldest daughter of Victoria Montalvo) spend their days with Benito's crafty partner, Vicente Rodríguez (formerly considered the Terror of the Coast), taking care of the money they've already earned, making arrangements for that which is yet to arrive.

Surprisingly, the ex-fisherman is very friendly with the duke (both apparently having ignored what supposedly happened in the cabin of *La Mariposa*), and the two spend many afternoons in the *mirador* of the villa, sipping sherry and listening to Vivaldi, often in the company of Benito's partner, sometimes with the mayor, once in a while with the priest.

Near sunset, however, Benito's son José (or sometimes José's beautiful wife, María) climbs into a new green Seat and drives Benito and Concepción to the shrine. There, the older couple, gray-haired, conservatively dressed, can be seen strolling hand in hand to the top of the hill, where, in the fading light, they gaze down at what was once the Peralta farm, then off across the hills at the fishing boats, sailing once again toward the open waters of the firth.